C000154144

Shady E

A Comedy

by Robin Hawdon

SAMUEL FRENCH

FOUNDED 1830

New York Hollywood London Toronto

SAMUELFRENCH.COM

ISBN 978-0-573-62257-1   Printed in U.S.A.   #21508

IMPORTANT BILLING AND CREDIT REQUIREMENTS

All producers of *SHADY BUSINESS must* give credit to the Author of the Play in all programs distributed in connection with performances of the Play and in all instances in which the title of the Play appears for purposes of advertising, publicizing or otherwise exploiting the Play and/or a production. The name of the Author *must* appear on a separate line on which no other name appears, immediately following the title, and *must* appear in size of type not less than fifty percent the size of the title type.

**First premiered in the United States at
Peninsular Players, Wisconsin, 2002.**

CAST

MANDY	a night-club dancer
GERRY	her boy-friend
TANIA	another dancer
TERRY	a lad-about-town
BIG MACK	a gang boss
DOZER	his side-kick
HARRY THE HAMMER	a loan shark

SETTING

The main living room of a smart London studio apartment. Stage Right the apartment door to the outside corridor. Upstage Centre the door to the kitchen. Stage Left the door to the bathroom. Upstage Right of Centre french widows to a balcony which continues Right off-stage. Upstage Left of Centre a double bed set back into an alcove. Downstage a sofa and an occasional chair.

The furnishings and personal belongings are feminine, frilly and rather gaudy, in contrast to the sophisticated architecture.

ACT I

(Morning. The sun streams in from the french windows through half-open curtains. Various clothes lie around the floor.
A male head emerges from the bed clothes and peers blearily round. Lifts the corner of the duvet beside him and reveals a blonde tousled head.)

GERRY. Morning.

(The head stirs sleepily.)

MANDY. Mmmm. Morning. *(She sits bolt upright.)* Morning! *(She is bright, pretty, a touch common, and totally guileless.)* Oh no! Oh my god, no!

GERRY. What? What's the matter?

MANDY. What's the time?

GERRY. *(Peering at his watch.)* Er.... Five to nine.

MANDY. Oh god - You shouldn't be here!

GERRY. Thanks a lot.

MANDY. It's Sunday morning!

GERRY. Are we going to church?

MANDY. No, you don't understand. You can't.... You mustn't....

GERRY. *(Pulling her to him.)* I already have.

5

MANDY. *(Resisting)* Gerry! Oh god, I should have told you.

GERRY. What?

MANDY. My situation. I shouldn't.... I can't.....

GERRY. *(Pulling her back.)* You already did.

MANDY. Gerry! This isn't funny. Big Mack will be here any moment.

GERRY. Big who?

MANDY. He always comes round on sundays to.... To....

GERRY. To what?

MANDY. To.... Oh you must go. He'll kill you if he finds you here!

GERRY. Who the hell's Big Mack?

MANDY. He's my.... My....

GERRY. What?

MANDY. Boss.

GERRY. Boss?

MANDY. He owns the club. He owns this apartment. He owns.... *(Waves her hands vaguely.)*

GERRY. You.

MANDY. Everything. He owns half London. And he'll do terrible things if he finds you here.

GERRY. Are you his girl?

MANDY. Well, sort of. Oh Gerry, it's been lovely, it really has. But you should have gone last night.

GERRY. I fell asleep.

MANDY. So did *I*. But we shouldn't have. I mean, we....

GERRY. Well we did have rather an exhausting time of it.

MANDY. Please, Gerry! Go, go! I don't want anything to happen to you.

GERRY. *(Pulling on his shorts beneath the bed-covers.)* Is he really that evil, this Big Mack guy?

MANDY. Not really. But he's very possessive and he's used to having his own way. I mean, he wouldn't kill you or anything. He'd just....

GERRY. What?

MANDY. Chop off some bits here and there.

GERRY. *(Jumping out of bed.)* Thanks a lot! *(Scurries about looking for his clothes.)* Why didn't you tell me about him?

MANDY. I didn't want you to.... Throw me that bath robe.

(He grabs an eye-dazzling frilly robe and holds it up for a second.)

GERRY. Good grief! *(Throws it to her.)*

MANDY. *(Putting it on.)* I liked you so much, Gerry. I didn't think you'd want me if you knew I was with him.

(He hops about putting on his trousers.)

GERRY. What's he do here at nine oclock on a Sunday, this Big Mack?

MANDY. Collects his money.

GERRY. His what?

MANDY. All the cash from his various clubs and.... things. It's all sent here at the end of the week, and he comes in the back way to collect it.

GERRY. Dirty money?

MANDY. Just cash, you know. Stuff the tax man won't know about.

GERRY. You mean he uses your place as a clearing shop?

MANDY. Well, it's his place really. He lets me have it as long as I keep quiet about what goes on.

GERRY And as long as you give him what he wants.

MANDY. Oh Gerry, he's not a bad man. He's been very kind to me. I'm just a little dancer from Essex. I could never have all this if I....

GERRY. Terrific! I've got myself involved with a gangster's chick!

MANDY. *(Running to him and flinging her arms round his neck.)* Please Gerry - don't be cross with me! Last night was so lovely. I didn't want to tell you in case....

GERRY. *(Pacifying)* All right, all right. Just find my shoes. While I've still got feet left to put in them. *(The door bell rings. They freeze.)* Oh my god!

MANDY. *(Running to pick up his shoes and socks.)* Quickly! Get dressed in the bathroom! *(Thrusts them at him and pushes him to the bathroom door.)* Lock the door!

GERRY. *(Turning at the door and kissing her.)* I really like you, Mandy. You shouldn't be involved with all this.

MANDY. *(Pushing him in.)* Quickly, quickly! I'll try and get rid of him.

(He goes into the bathroom with his various bits of clothing. She goes towards the apartment door. Sees a sock lying on the floor. Picks it up and hurls it into the bathroom. The door bell rings again. She hurries to the door and opens it. TANIA stands there. Dark, elegant, cool.)

TANIA. 'Morning, sweetie.
MANDY. Tania!
TANIA. Need a hand with the totting up this morning?
MANDY. Thank god it's you! Come in, quickly!

(Ushers TANIA in and closes the door.)

TANIA. What's up?

MANDY. I thought it might be Big Mack.

TANIA. Don't tell me he rings the bell?

MANDY. Well he sometimes sends one of his boys.

TANIA. You shouldn't be doing this, Mandy. All this money lying around your place on a Sunday morning. It'll end in tears.

MANDY. I know. Oh, Tania - you remember I told you I met someone last night at the club?

TANIA. You told me a man tried to pick you up.

MANDY. He did pick me up. But he's not the usual sort.

TANIA. They're all the usual sort.

MANDY. It's all right for you, Tania. You're in love. You've found your feller.

TANIA. Ah well, it's early days. You've never got a man until you've got him into bed.

MANDY. I hope you're right.

TANIA. And you don't do that too soon or he'll think you're cheap.

MANDY. I hope you're wrong.

TANIA. What? Don't tell me.....

MANDY. Yes.

TANIA. Last night?

MANDY. He's still here.

TANIA. Where?

MANDY. In the bathroom. *(Goes to the bathroom door and calls through it.)* Gerry, it's all right, it's only Tania. Another dancer from the club.

TANIA. He spent the whole night here?

MANDY. Yes. Everything happened like you dream about.

TANIA. *(Hopelessly)* Oh, Mandy....

MANDY. If it hadn't been your night off you'd have met him.

He's lovely, Tania.

TANIA. He won't stay lovely if Big Mack finds out.

MANDY. No, I.... *(Tries the handle. It's locked.)* Gerry, hurry up. You must get out of here. *(No response. She knocks on the door.)* What are you doing in there? *(To TANIA.)* There's no answer.

TANIA. *(Dry)* Perhaps you've given him a heart attack.

MANDY. Don't joke. (Knocks) Gerry, please! Hurry up!

TANIA. Must have worked fast last night.

MANDY. We just had a drink together after the show.

TANIA. Against the rules, Mandy.

MANDY. I know. But we talked and talked.... And one thing led to another, and....

TANIA. Another, and another. You're a fool.

MANDY. We just.... felt right - you know.

TANIA. Who is he?

MANDY. He's quite posh. Works in the city somewhere. Makes lots of lolly.

TANIA. And treats you as one of his bonuses. He's just taking advantage of you, Mandy.

MANDY. No, it wasn't like that - really. He.... *(The telephone rings. MANDY jumps.)* Oh god! *(Answers it.)* Yes? Yes, Fred. Who is he? Well, send him up. *(Looks at the bathroom.)* No, no! Keep him there, Fred, I, er.... *(Dithers)* Oh lord! Look, I'm coming down. What? Well stop him. I'm on my way. *(Puts the phone down.)* Fred's got another delivery at reception for me. Look, Tania, I'll just pop down and stop whoever it is coming up.

TANIA. You're not dressed.

MANDY. *(Indicates the bathroom.)* I can't - all my clothes are in there! You stay here and see Gerry gets away quickly, will you?

TANIA. I don't see how I can help.

MANDY. Please, Tania! *(Hurries to the dressing table and brushes her hair.)* And listen - if Big Mack or anyone gets here before I'm back, say he's with you.

TANIA. Who?

MANDY. Gerry! In there! Say he belongs to you.

TANIA. Who's going to believe that?

MANDY. Say you both dropped in for coffee. You are my neighbour after all.

TANIA. But I've already got a man. I'm just not as quick at getting his trousers off as you are!

MANDY. *(Putting on shoes.)* They don't know who he is.

TANIA. He's coming here for the week-end. This is the big test. What am I going to tell him if there's someone else around?

MANDY. Gerry'll be gone by then.

TANIA. But what if Big Mack then meets Larry?

MANDY. Who?

TANIA. My feller!

MANDY. Say this one's a reject.

TANIA. He'll think I'm running a stud farm.

MANDY. Please Tania!

TANIA. *(Sighing)* It'll end in tears.

MANDY. *(Banging on the bathroom door.)* Please, Gerry, hurry up! We haven't much time. *(Hurries to the apartment door. Turns.)* Save him from Big Mack, Tania. He's a lovely boy - you'll like him.

(Goes, leaving the door ajar.)

TANIA. I knew I should never have come to London. *(Knocks on the bathroom door.)* Hey, lover boy. You'd better get your skates on, or your dancing-girl days are numbered. *(No answer. She frowns.)* **I'll go and put some coffee on. Sounds as if you need it.**

*(Goes into the kitchen. The door swings shut behind her. Slight
    pause. The bathroom door opens cautiously. GERRY sticks his
    head out. At that moment the apartment door is pushed open,
    and TERRY sticks his head in.)*

      TERRY. Hello? *(GERRY hurriedly retreats back into the bath-
room, closing the door. TERRY hears the sound and comes in. He
is a London wise boy, snappily dressed.)* **Anyone at home?**

*(Goes to the bathroom door and tries the handle. TANIA comes out
    of the kitchen.)*

      TANIA. Ah!
      TERRY. *(Jumping)* Ah!
      TANIA. You've appeared.
      TERRY. Sorry - I, er....
      TANIA. What were you doing? Trying on all her wigs?
      TERRY. I was just, er.... Who are you?
      TANIA. I'm Tania from down the passage.
      TERRY. Oh I know you! You're in the show.
      TANIA. Yes.
      TERRY. *(Flirty)* I've seen it. Great line of legs.
      TANIA. Well keep your sights on one pair at a time, boyo!
      TERRY. *(Taken aback.)* Er... Where's Mandy?
      TANIA. Gone downstairs for a sec.
      TERRY. Oh. I've missed her.
      TANIA. Already? How touching.
      TERRY. *(Puzzled)* Yeh, er.... Look, I've made a bit of a balls
up here.

TANIA. You can say that again. Big Mack's due here any moment for his deliveries, and your balls could be up your backside.

TERRY. I realise that. I should have given her one last night, you see.

TANIA. You did pretty well from what I've heard.

TERRY. No, no, I got side-tracked.

TANIA. Did you?

TERRY. I wasn't concentrating on the business in hand. I should have come quickly. In and out, and away again smartish.

TANIA. Charming!

TERRY. But I couldn't manage it. I had a problem.

TANIA. She wasn't complaining.

TERRY. Well nevertheless that's why I'm here now. I had to put things right this morning.

TANIA. Real gentleman, aren't you?

TERRY. Sorry? No, you don't understand.

TANIA. I think I do.

TERRY. I wanted to explain. I didn't want her to think I'd just swanned over here to shove it through her slot and then bugger off again.

TANIA. Delicate turn of phrase you have, Gerry.

TERRY. Terry.

TANIA. Terry?

TERRY. Yeh.

TANIA. Oh, I thought she said Gerry.

TERRY. *(Puzzled)* No. Look, what do you know about all this anyway?

TANIA. Only what she's told me. Which is quite enough.

TERRY. I didn't realise she'd be so concerned.

TANIA. *(Shaking her head.)* You men! Always got other irons in the fire, haven't you?

TERRY. Oh, of course you work at the club, don't you? I suppose you hear everything that goes on there.

TANIA. I get to know most things, sooner or later. Just pray Big Mack doesn't.

TERRY. Yeh, right.

(BIG MACK walks in carrying a brief case. He is followed by DOZER, who is even bigger.)

MACK. Just pray Big Mack doesn't what, Tania girl?

TANIA. Oh Mack - good morning.

MACK. *(Inspecting TERRY.)* Who's this? And what's he praying for?

TERRY. I'm, er....

TANIA. *(Quickly)* He's my boy friend, Mack.

TERRY. Eh?

TANIA. Terry.

MACK. Terry?

TANIA. Yes. *(Taking TERRY'S arm.)* He's new.

MACK. He looks a bit surprised. Have you told him yet?

TANIA. *(False laugh.)* It's supposed to be a secret. Isn't it, darling?

TERRY. Definitely.

TANIA. We met at the club. That's what you weren't supposed to know, Mack.

MACK. Ah. I see.

TANIA. We just dropped in for a cup of coffee with Mandy.

MACK. So you picked her up at the club, did you, Terry? Against the rules, that.

TERRY. Sorry. I didn't realise I had.

MACK. Had what?

TERRY. Er... Broken the rules.

MACK. Tania should have told you.

TANIA. Yes, I should. But these things happen, Mack.

MACK. Yes. Well we'll overlook it as long as you're nice to her, Terry. My girls are special to me, and I like to know they're in safe hands. Know what I mean?

TERRY. Yeh - absolutely.

(MACK indicates his side-kick.)

MACK. This here's Dozer.

TERRY. Dozer?

MACK. As in 'bull'.

(Hands DOZER his brief case.)

TERRY. Ah. *(To DOZER.)* How d'you do.

(DOZER nods.)

MACK. He doesn't say a lot. He just bulldozers. When needed. *(TERRY laughs feebly.)* Where's Mandy?

TANIA. She went downstairs. To see if there were any more deliveries.

MACK. Ah. Must have missed her. We came up the back way. Always best never to let people know quite where you're coming from - know what I mean, Terry?

TERRY. Yeh.

MACK. That way you always find out if anyone's trespassing too far onto your territory. Understand what I'm saying, Terry?

TERRY. Yeh.
MACK. Good boy.

(MANDY hurries in.)

MANDY. Oh, Mack - you're here.
MACK. Hello, Mandy darling. Give your Uncle Mack a Sunday morning kiss. *(She kisses him.)* You're not dressed yet.
MANDY. No.... I overslept.
MACK. I've just been meeting Terry here.
MANDY. Terry?
TANIA. *(Quickly)* My new boy friend.
MANDY. Boy friend?
TANIA. *(Nodding at the bathroom door.)* I told you about him.
MANDY. That's not him!
TANIA. What?
MACK. What?
MANDY. *(Caught)* I mean.... That's not who I thought it was.
MACK. Who did you think it was?
MANDY. Er.... Someone else.
MACK. Someone else?
MANDY. A different boy friend.
MACK. How many boy friends you got, Tania?
TANIA. Er.... One or two.
MACK. What does Terry think of that?
TANIA. Oh, he's very broad-minded - aren't you, Terry?
TERRY. *(Still bemused.)* Yeh.
MACK. Well don't get too broad-minded, Terry. Not the best way to start a relationship, that. If I found Mandy here was two-timing me I'd probably kill 'em both. *(To MANDY.)* Wouldn't I, love?

MANDY. Yes, Mack.

MACK. Right. Where's the week's takings?

MANDY. Usual place. In the fridge.

MACK. *(To TERRY.)* Always best to keep hot money cool, eh Terry?

TERRY. Yeh.

MACK. Only you never heard any of that.

TERRY. No.

MACK. *(Going towards the kitchen.)* All the envelopes arrived, have they?

MANDY. Um.... I think so.

TERRY. Oh, well I er....

MACK. *(Stopping)* What?

TERRY. *(Looking from him to TANIA.)* Nothing.

MACK. You keep out of this, son. It's none of your business.

TERRY. Right.

MACK. You stand guard, Dozer, while I go and count up.

(DOZER nods and stands by the kitchen door as MACK goes in. The door closes behind him.)

MANDY. *(Aghast, pointing at TERRY.)* Who...? *(She wavers, looking from DOZER to TERRY. Goes to DOZER and wheedles up to him.)* Dozer, you've always been my friend, haven't you?

DOZER. Mmmm.

MANDY. You wouldn't do anything to get me into trouble, would you?

DOZER. Depends.

MANDY. Please, Dozer! We've got a bit of a difficult situation here. Don't say anything to Big Mack. You know he gets the wrong end of the stick sometimes. *(Strokes his chest.)* Please, Dozer.

DOZER. *(Grudging)* S'long as it's not serious.

MANDY. 'Course it's not. It's just.... a muddle. *(Strokes his cheek.)* I'll let you wash my back in the bath again. *(DOZER grins sheepishly.)* Tania will let you wash her back too. Won't you, tania?

TANIA. Bloody hell!

MANDY. All right, Dozer?

DOZER. *(Sheepish)* All right.

(MANDY goes to TANIA and TERRY, who have been watching, bewildered. She whispers fiercely.)

MANDY. Right - who the hell is this?

TANIA. It's your feller.

MANDY. It certainly is not my feller!

TANIA. *(To TERRY.)* Aren't you her feller?

TERRY. *(Shaking his head.)* I'm not her feller.

MANDY. *(Indicating the bathroom.)* I told you to get rid of that one in there, not go out and get another one!

TANIA. He is that one in there.

MANDY. How can he be that one in there?

TANIA. I saw him come out of there. *(To TERRY.)* Didn't I see you come out of there?

TERRY. No, you saw me going in there.

TANIA. What for?

TERRY. To see who else was in there.

TANIA. I'm going out of my mind! Who else was in there?

TERRY. Don't ask me. *(Indicates the front door.)* I came in there, and someone else was going in there. *(Indicates the bathroom.)*

TANIA. *(To MANDY.)* Who else could be in there?

MANDY. The one I told you was in there!

TANIA. Well where is he now?

MANDY. Still in there, I presume.

TANIA. *(Going to the bathroom.)* He can't be! *(Tries the door.)* He is.

MANDY. *(Pushing her aside and whispering through the door.)* Gerry!

TANIA. I thought she said Gerry.

MANDY. Will you come out of there, for christ's sake! *(Turns)* He must have climbed out the window.

TANIA. Four stories up?

MANDY. This is ridiculous. *(Indicating TERRY.)* Who's this then?

TERRY. I'm Terry.

MANDY. Terry?

TANIA. I thought he was your guy. So I told Big Mack he was mine - like you said.

MANDY. Terrific! Where'd he come from?

TANIA. I don't know.

TERRY. Luigi's.

TANIA. Luigi's?

MANDY. Oh! You're the one Fred said was downstairs! I just missed you.

TERRY. The lift was busy, so I took the stairs.

TANIA. You mean you're one of the firm?

TERRY. *(Nodding)* I'm new. My boss runs the restaurant for Big Mack. He told me to deliver the week's.... You know, dosh.

MANDY. That should have come last night.

TERRY. I had a bit of bother.

MANDY. Bother?

TERRY. I couldn't come over then. So I came this morning. To try and explain.

MANDY. Explain what?

(He takes an envelope from his pocket, and glances at DOZER.)

TERRY. *(Whispering)* This is it. But it's not all there.
MANDY. Not all there!
TERRY. Shhh! I lost some.
MANDY. Lost?
TERRY. Yeh.
MANDY. Where?
TERRY. At your club.
MANDY. How?
TERRY. Playing roulette.
MANDY. What??
TERRY. There's an illegal gaming room round the back.
MANDY. I know that. What were you doing there?
TERRY. I went there.... For a flutter.
MANDY. How much did you lose?
TERRY. A grand.
MANDY. A thousand quid!
TANIA. From Luigi's takings?
TERRY. Yeh.
MANDY. Bloody hell, Terry! You went gambling at Big Mack's club with Big Mack's own money?
TERRY. Yeh.
MANDY. He's cut off ears for less than that!
TERRY. I know, but you see I had a bit of a crisis.
TANIA. You've got a bigger one now.
TERRY. The thing was, I owed some money, and it had to be paid back.
MANDY. How much?

TERRY. A thousand quid.
TANIA. Another thousand?
TERRY. Yeh.
MANDY. Who to?
TERRY. Er.... Big Mack actually.

(Pause)

MANDY. Can you start again?

TERRY. It was like this. A few weeks ago I wanted some cash to make up the price on this car a mate of mine was selling. Great little sports car. So I borrowed a grand from a loan shark - stupid, I know - who turned out to be one of Big Mack's people.

TANIA. Name?

TERRY. Harry the Hammer, they called him.

MANDY. Oh god!

TERRY. Then I lost my job, and I couldn't keep up the payments. I spent everything I had on the interest alone....

MANDY. Why didn't you go to a bank? - they'll give you interest in single figures.

TERRY. I'm already over my limit there.

MANDY. Silly question.

TERRY. Anyway, this Harry character was coming on heavy for his thousand quid back - or Big Mack's as it turns out.

TANIA. That's why he's called the Hammer. Flattens your parts.

TERRY. Yeh. Well then by chance I got the job at Luigi's, and found out that was one of Big Mack's businesses too, and suddenly I had an idea.

MANDY. Oh dear.

TERRY. I thought, if I used some of his cash to gamble at his own club, then I might win enough to pay him back his thousand,

and if I didn't, well it wouldn't matter too much because he'd only be winning back his own money.... If you see what I mean.

(Long pause.)

MANDY. What?

TERRY. Well, it seemed to make sense at the time.

TANIA. *(Slowly)* Let me get this straight. You gambled at Big Mack's club, with Big Mack's money, to try and win from Big Mack money you owed Big Mack, thinking that if you lost it to Big Mack it was Big Mack's anyway, so Big Mack wouldn't mind?

(Pause)

TERRY. Yeh.

(TANIA looks slowly round at DOZER.)

TANIA. What do you think about that, Dozer?

DOZER. *(Frowning)* Sounds all right to me.

TANIA. I somehow don't think it'll sound all right to Big Mack.

MANDY. It'll sound bloody unbelievable to Big Mack! Big Mack will have Harry hammer your parts so flat you'll never find them again.

TANIA. Why didn't you stop when you knew you were losing?

TERRY. I put it all on in one go.

MANDY. All at once?

TERRY. *(Nodding)* I figured it was fifty-fifty to double it and solve the problem. So I put it all on the red. It's my lucky colour.

MANDY. Your lucky colour.

TERRY. Well, not this time.

TANIA. Red's the colour of blood, Terry. You now owe Big Mack two thousand pounds, and he's going to know about it any moment.

TERRY. Not my best day, is it?

MANDY. Right - I've got to come up with something fast.

TERRY. Oh, yes please!

MANDY. Not for you, for me.

TERRY. Oh.

MANDY. Your problem's beyond help. I've got my own.

TERRY. Yeh, what was all that - me being her boy-friend?

MANDY. Mind your own business.

TANIA. It is his business. Mine too now. I've got one wrong boy friend, one lost boy-friend, and one boy-friend about to come out of the bathroom.

MANDY. *(To DOZER.)* You haven't heard any of this remember, Dozer.

DOZER. I don't understand any of it anyway.

MANDY. Good. *(Turning back.)* Right, now....

(BIG MACK sticks his head out of the kitchen.)

MACK. Dozer, I need a hand with this. Come in here.

DOZER. Yes, boss.

(The other three have frozen stiff. MACK notices them.)

MACK. What's the matter with you lot? Stuck on freeze-frame?

MANDY. *(Feebly)* We're er.... Doing a charade for Dozer.

MACK. What is it - 'Olympic highlights'?

(Laughs at his own joke and disappears, followed by DOZER.)

MANDY. Right, you and Terry go back to your place and work out where to find a thousand quid to put back in that envelope. I'll stay here and do something about this idiot in the bathroom.

TANIA. Lovely feller, you called him.

MANDY. Well he won't be lovely much longer if I can't get him out of there. Now go. *(To TERRY.)* Just a minute. Give me the envelope. *(He does so.)* How much is in here?

TERRY. Eleven grand. Should be twelve.

MANDY. Right - go, go. *(They leave. MANDY shuts the apartment door behind them, glances at the kitchen, goes to the bathroom door and taps.)* Gerry? Gerry, are you there? You'll have to come out sometime. *(The door opens slowly, and GERRY looks cautiously out.)* Oh, thank god! I thought you'd died in there.

GERRY. Sorry.

MANDY. What were you doing - trying to get out through the plug-hole?

GERRY. Hiding.

MANDY. Who from, Big Mack?

GERRY. No.

MANDY. Dozer?

GERRY. No.

MANDY. Then who?

GERRY. Tania.

MANDY. Tania?

GERRY. Yes.

MANDY. Why?

GERRY. I'm her new boy-friend.

(Pause)

MANDY. Her boy-friend's not here yet.

GERRY. Yes, he is.

MANDY. He's called Larry.

GERRY. I'm called Larry.

MANDY. You said Gerry.

LARRY. So you wouldn't know I was Larry.

MANDY. Oh my god! Is this for real? *(He nods.)* How did it happen?

LARRY. I'd been out with Tania a couple of times, and then on my first visit to the club I saw you in the show.

MANDY. I thought things were really hotting up between you two.

LARRY. They were for her, but I.... Well she's a great girl, but a bit too powerful for me - know what I mean?

MANDY. Typical man. Can't take a girl with a mind of her own.

LARRY. But then I saw you and I couldn't take my eyes off you. That's my kind of girl, I thought.

MANDY. Thought I didn't have a mind of my own?

LARRY. No, no, not at all. I just couldn't get you out of my mind. So I came to London a day early this week-end, and went to see the show again, knowing it was Tania's night off. And then I met you after. And then one thing led to another, and.... Well you know the rest.

MANDY. Oh my god, Gerry....

LARRY. Larry.

MANDY. She's my best friend. What am I going to tell her?

LARRY. What am I going to tell her? I feel a shit.

MANDY. Why didn't you tell me?

LARRY. I am telling you.

MANDY. At the start.

LARRY. I knew you wouldn't talk to me then. I had to do it, Mandy. I'd never felt like that at first sight of a girl before.

MANDY. Oh, Gerry....

LARRY. Larry.

MANDY. Larry. *(They hug each other.)* Did you hear everything through the door?

LARRY. (Nodding) She picked the wrong bloke. Big help.

MANDY. Well, at least she didn't see you. Let's get you out of here before they catch you.

(They go towards the apartment door. MANDY opens it to reveal TERRY, about to knock. He enters.)

TERRY. Oh look, I.... *(Sees LARRY)* Oh, is this the one in the bathroom?

MANDY. Yeh.

TERRY. Who is he?

MANDY. Mind your own business.

TERRY. Right. I want to talk to you about that envelope.

MANDY. Not here, Terry. Big Mack'll be out any minute.

LARRY. I'd better go.

(Heads for the door.)

MANDY. *(To TERRY)* Where's Tania?

TERRY. Waiting by the lift to catch her bloke.

(LARRY does a smart about-turn in the doorway.)

LARRY. P'raps not just yet.
TERRY. She doesn't want him running into Big Mack.
MANDY. No, she wouldn't.
TERRY. Has he got money problems too?
MANDY. No, identity problems. Big Mack thinks you're him.
TERRY. Oh yeh. Great.

(LARRY'S mobile phone rings.)

MANDY. Shhh!

(He answers it urgently.)

LARRY. Yes? Oh, yes, love. I'm, er.... Just around the corner. Yeh - I got here early. Can't talk now, sweetheart. See you in a sec. *(Switches off the phone. Grins feebly at the other two.)* My other bird. Wants to know where I am.

TERRY. Good job she doesn't know, by the sound of it.
LARRY. Yeh. *(To MANDY.)* What shall I do?
MANDY. *(Going to the french windows.)* Nip out here for the moment. I'll bring you in when it's safe.
TERRY. Why should he....?
MANDY. Mind your own business.
TERRY. Right.

(She hands LARRY the envelope as he passes.)

MANDY. Take this with you. And keep out of sight of the kitchen.

(LARRY disappears along the balcony. MANDY turns to TERRY.)

TERRY. What....?

MANDY. Mind your own business.

TERRY. Right.

MANDY. Just remember, if you want our help you're still Tania's feller for now.

TERRY. Right.

MANDY. Now what were you saying about the envelope?

TERRY. I was going to say, don't give it to Big Mack yet.

MANDY. I haven't.

TERRY. No, well I've been thinking - it's better he doesn't get one at all for the moment, than he gets one that's short.

MANDY. But what am I going to tell him? He'll soon notice it's missing.

TERRY. He may not.

(BIG MACK sticks his head out of the kitchen.)

MACK. Here, Mandy, there's an envelope missing.

(MANDY just looks at TERRY.)

MANDY. *(Innocently)* Is there, Mack?

MACK. From Luigi's.

MANDY. That's funny.

MACK. *(Seeing TERRY.)* You still here then?

TERRY. Er.... Yeh - just going.

MACK. You're not listening to this.

TERRY. Right.

MACK. *(To MANDY.)* Didn't it come last night?

MANDY. I didn't notice, Mack. Isn't it with the others?

MACK. No. Ten outfits, nine envelopes. You're supposed to count them, Mandy.

MANDY. Sorry.

MACK. Give Luigi a call and ask him what's happened.

MANDY. Right.

MACK. *(To TERRY.)* You didn't hear that.

TERRY. Right. *(MACK goes back into the kitchen.)* Luigi's my boss. He'll kill me.

MANDY. Well, you've got a choice - either he'll kill you, or Big Mack'll kill you. Which would you rather?

TERRY. Just don't tell my boss you've seen me.

MANDY. They'll think you've scarpered with the lot.

TERRY. Oh god - how did I get into this?

MANDY. Fast cars and casinos, Terry. Old, old story. How did I get into it, more's the point.

TERRY. Fast men and libidos by the sound of it.

MANDY. Yeh, right.

(TANIA appears in the doorway.)

TANIA. I don't understand. I just called Larry on his mobile. He's here already. I was going to warn him not to come up, but he cut me off. He sounded very odd.

MANDY. Odd?

TANIA. As if he didn't want to talk to me.

MANDY. Probably hurrying to get to you.

TANIA. Where's the one in the bathroom?

MANDY. Gone.

TANIA. Gone?

MANDY. Yes.

TANIA. Nobody passed me.

MANDY. I sent him down the back stairs.

TERRY. I thought he was....

MANDY. Shut up!

TERRY. Right.

TANIA. What was he doing in there?

MANDY. Sleeping.

TANIA. Sleeping?

MANDY. In the bath. *(False laugh.)* I wore him out.

TANIA. Good grief! *(To TERRY.)* Did you tell her about holding onto the envelope?

TERRY. Yes.

TANIA. *(To MANDY.)* Where is it now?

MANDY. I've hidden it.

TANIA. Where?

MANDY. In the bed.

TERRY. I thought you'd....

MANDY. Shut up!

TERRY. Right.

TANIA. What's the matter with him?

MANDY. He keeps jumping to conclusions.

TANIA. Funny about that call though. He said he was just around the corner.

MANDY. Then you'd better go and meet him.

TERRY. Just a minute....

TANIA. What?

TERRY. You just phoned him?

TANIA. Yes.

TERRY. Your boy friend?

TANIA. Yes.

TERRY. The one I was supposed to be?

MANDY. Terry....

TANIA. Yes.

TERRY. And he was just around the corner?

MANDY. Terry....

TANIA. Yes. What's up?

TERRY. *(Looking at MANDY.)* Bloody hell!

MANDY. Now Terry....

TERRY. The penny's dropped. You lot don't half put it about, don't you?

TANIA. What the hell are you talking about?

MANDY. He's just clicked that he's up the spout if Larry shows up.

TERRY. Or he's down the toilet.

MANDY. Terry....

TERRY. Or p'raps out the window.

MANDY. Terry! *(Kicks him in the shins.)*

TERRY. Ow!

TANIA. What on earth....?

(MACK comes out of the kitchen, followed by DOZER. They all freeze in strange positions.)

MACK. What's this one - Superbowl? Ha, ha. *(To MANDY.)* Have you talked to Luigi?

MANDY. I was just going to.

(She goes to the phone.)

MACK. *(To the other two,)* You two seem to like it here.

TANIA. Sorry, Mack. We don't want to intrude on your business.

MACK. What business?

TERRY. Your business with.... *(MACK just looks at him.)* I dunno - what business?

MANDY. *(On the phone.)* Luigi? Er.... Big Mack wants a word with you.

(MACK takes the phone.)

MACK. Luigi? What's happened to this week's envelope? It's not here. Last night? Who d'you give it to? The new boy. Was that wise, Luigi? How much was in it? Well, if he's scarpered with it I'm going to strangle you both - with his intestines. *(TERRY nearly passes out. MACK puts down the phone.)* You sure no-one's been around here, Mandy girl? No new face?

MANDY. Er.... No, Mack. I've not seen anyone.

MACK. I don't understand it. Why would anyone risk his life for a mere twelve grand?

TANIA. *(Glancing at TERRY.)* Some would risk it for a lot less than that.

MACK. Well he'd better show up with it soon, or he's dead mutton.

TERRY. *(Weak)* If he's new, perhaps he got lost.

MACK. *(Turning to him.)* Who got lost?

TERRY. *(Quickly)* Nobody.

MACK. Better educate your boy friend, Tania girl - before he becomes your ex boy friend.

TANIA. Yes, Mack.

MACK. And if I were you I'd have a look through your other boy friends and see if there isn't one more suitable.

TANIA. Yes, Mack.

(LARRY appears in the french windows, peering in. MANDY waves him back.)

MACK. *(Turning)* By the way, Mandy girl.... *(She hurriedly stops waving.)* Where were you last night after the show? I was looking for you.

MANDY. *(Innocently)* Were you, Mack?

MACK. Where'd you get to?

MANDY. I.... Came home early.

MACK. You always say goodnight.

MANDY. I couldn't see you anywhere, and I was so tired.

MACK. Weren't fraternising with any of the clients, or anything like that, were you? You know that's not allowed.

MANDY. 'Course not, Mack.

MACK. *(Handing her a wad of notes.)* Well put this cash in your hand-bag, Mandy darling, and keep it safe for tonight.

MANDY. Tonight?

MACK. We're free tonight, being Sunday, so you and I are taking Harry the Hammer and his missus out on the town. *(TERRY nearly faints again.)* It's their anniversary.

MANDY. How many years?

MACK. Only one, but that's a record for Harry. It's his fifth marriage.

MANDY. *(Taking the money.)* Right, Mack.

MACK. Unless that is, that other envelope doesn't show up, and Dozer and me have something more important to do.

MANDY. Yes, Mack.

(He goes back towards the kitchen.)

MACK. We've nearly done counting. Good haul this week.
MANDY. Good.

(He stops at the door and turns.)

MACK. You'd never believe it. Some young wally came into the club last night for a flutter at roulette, and put a grand on the red. All in one go.

MANDY. No!

MACK. Yes. How stupid can you get?

TANIA. So naturally they made sure he lost?

MACK. Naturally. *(TANIA just looks at TERRY, who nearly chokes. MACK looks at him.)* What did I just say then?

TERRY. *(Hoarse)* I didn't hear a thing.

MACK. Well done.

(Exits to the kitchen, followed by DOZER.)

TERRY. Oh god I'm stupid!

MANDY. Yes.

TERRY. I'm not sure I'm going to survive this.

TANIA. Well you'd better, chum, because if you don't, I won't. And neither will my new feller probably.

(LARRY appears in the french windows again. MANDY gestures to him to come in from the balcony.)

MANDY. *(Moving downstage to distract TANIA and TERRY.)* Why? He's no part of this, is he?

(LARRY inches open the french windows behind their backs, slips through, and side-steps cautiously towards the apartment door.)

TANIA. We're all part of this if Mack finds out. You've got rid of your man, but how am I going to explain I'm running two?

TERRY. I could break off our relationship.

TANIA. Oh shut up!

TERRY. Right.

TANIA. Where's Larry got to anyway? *(She turns just in time to catch LARRY in the apartment doorway, about to vanish.)* Ah, there you are!

LARRY. *(Beaming cheerfully.)* Ah, there you are!

TANIA. You've got here early.

LARRY. Yes, I er.... Couldn't keep away.

TANIA. Well this is not a good time to arrive, sweetheart. Come back to my flat.

LARRY. Why, what's up? *(Indicating the other two.)* Who's this?

TERRY. I'm her....

TANIA. Shut up!

TERRY. Right.

TANIA. This is Mandy - my friend.

MANDY. Hello.

LARRY. Oh, yes - I've seen you in the show.

TANIA. *(Nodding at TERRY.)* You don't need to know about him.

TERRY. Thanks.

TANIA. And my boss is in the kitchen with his heavy. They don't need to know about you.

LARRY. *(Innocently)* Why not?

(He notices his tie, still draped over the sofa.)

TANIA. It's complicated. I'll explain later. Let's go.

LARRY. Yes, right. *(Pointedly, for MANDY'S benefit.)* As long as there's no ties here.

TANIA. *(Puzzled)* Ties?

LARRY. Yes. Nothing to 'tie' us here.

TANIA. What d'you mean?

LARRY. Well, since we're quite 'tied' up together....

TANIA. Tied up?

LARRY. *(Glaring furiously at the tie.)* I wouldn't want there to be any 'ties' anywhere else - know what I mean?

TANIA. What the hell are you blathering about?

TERRY. He seems to be tongue-tied - ha,ha.

TANIA. Don't you start!

(MANDY finally cottons on, grabs the tie from the sofa, and stuffs it under a cushion.)

MANDY. No ties here, Larry.

LARRY. *(Relieved)* Right. Let's go then.

(MACK enters, followed by DOZER with the brief-case.)

MACK. Right, well that's....*(They all freeze.)* It's like Madame Tussaud's in here! *(Sees LARRY.)* And who the bloody hell's this?

LARRY. Er....

MANDY. Er.... He's the new boy.

MACK. New boy?

MANDY. From Luigi's. He's turned up.

TANIA. Oh, great.

MACK. What?

TANIA. Nothing.

MACK. *(To LARRY.)* You're Luigi's lad?

LARRY. Um.... *(TANIA and MANDY nod furiously.)* Yes.

MACK. Where the sodding hell you been?

LARRY. I, er....
MANDY. He had a bit of bother.
MACK. Bother?
MANDY. He got tied up.
TERRY. *(Nodding)* Yes.
MACK. What?
TERRY. Nothing.
MACK. *(To LARRY.)* You got my envelope?
MANDY. Yes. Give it to him, Larry.
MACK. That your name?
LARRY. Yes.
MACK. *(Holding out his hand.)* Well, Larry?
LARRY. Yeh. *(Takes the envelope from his pocket.)* There.
MACK. Good boy. Better late than never.
TANIA. *(Bewildered)* How on earth....?
MACK. What?
TANIA. Nothing.
MACK. This is none of your business, Tania girl.
TANIA. No, Mack. *(MACK sees TERRY staring at the envelope.)* Or yours.
 TERRY. Me? No - what business?

(MACK turns to DOZER.)

 MACK. Right, Dozer. I've got a bit more counting to do. *(Points at the apartment door.)* Don't let any of this lot leave until I'm done, right?
 DOZER. Yes, boss.
 MACK. Something smells a bit funny round here. *(Nose to nose with TERRY.)* And it's not your after-shave.

(Goes)

TANIA. *(To LARRY)* How did you....?
LARRY. What?
TANIA. Get that envelope?
LARRY. I, er....

(Looks desperately at MANDY.)

TERRY. I can tell you.
MANDY. *(Quickly)* No, you can't. *(To TANIA.)* I arranged it.
TANIA. How?
MANDY. Well.... *(Looks at DOZER.)* You're not listening to this, Dozer.
DOZER. I'll try not.
MANDY. When I got my guy Gerry out of here, I realised we had a problem, because you had said Terry was Gerry. So I thought Larry had better be Terry. And I gave Gerry the money, and told him to look for Larry, and tell him to pretend to be Terry. So Gerry found Larry in the lobby, and told him he was now Terry, and gave him the lolly. So now all we've got to remember is that Terry is Larry, and Larry is Terry, and Gerry's not here. That's right, isn't it Larry?
LARRY. Yes.
MANDY. *(To DOZER.)* Did you understand that, Dozer?
DOZER. *(After thinking about it.)* No.
MANDY. Good.
TANIA. I see.
TERRY. Hang on. I thought this Gerry was really....
MANDY. *(Interrupting)* You think too much, that's your problem, Terry. It's going to get you into a lot of trouble one of these days.

TERRY. Yeh, right.

TANIA. Well, what the hell are we going to do now?

MANDY. Why?

TANIA. No-one's who they say they are, and that envelope's a grand short, and my date's going to get the blame for it.

LARRY. Terrific!

MANDY. Has anyone got a thousand quid on them?

TERRY. Preferably two.

MANDY. Dozer?

DOZER. I've got a tenner.

MANDY. Thanks. Well your boss is going to come out of there in a minute in a very bad mood. Unless we can think of something.

TERRY. I've thought of something.

MANDY. What?

TERRY. How much did Big Mack give you just now?

MANDY. When?

TERRY. When he said you and he were taking Harry the Hammer out on the town.

MANDY. Terry - I hope you're not thinking what I think you're thinking.

TERRY. Well it looked quite a lot.

MANDY. It was quite a lot. Mack likes to live it up when he goes out.

TERRY. I was just wondering....

MANDY. Well don't wonder. That sort of wondering can get you into real trouble. Anyway, it wouldn't be as much as a grand.

DOZER. It is.

MANDY. What?

TERRY. What?

DOZER. It's a grand. He had me count it.

MANDY. Dozer! Are you trying to get us all shot?

DOZER. *(Shrugging)* I was just telling you.

TERRY. You see, it would give us a bit more time.

MANDY. Are you out of your mind? You're already going to get done for thieving from him, Larry's going to get done because he'll think it was him thieving from him, and now you want me to get done for thieving from him again!

TERRY. *(Shrugging)* Might as well get hung for a sheep as a lamb.

MANDY. It depends what part of you you get hung from! Anyway, he's got the envelope. How could I get it back in there?

LARRY. Give it to me.

MANDY. What?

LARRY. I'm the one he'll come after for it. I should be the one to give it to him.

MANDY. How will you do that?

LARRY. I'll think of something. Quick! Give it to me.

MANDY. (Opening her bag.) And what do I do when he comes after me for it?

LARRY. We'll think of something else.

(BIG MACK enters, carrying the envelope. MANDY hands LARRY the cash behind her back just in time.)

MACK. Here, you, new boy - there's....

LARRY. *(Interrupting)* Oh, Mack, there's another thousand quid to go in there....

MACK. I know.

LARRY. Here it is.

(Holds out the money.)

MACK. *(Staring at it.)* How come?

LARRY. Er.... My boss gave it to me at the last minute as I was leaving. Said it was extra. I forgot I had it in my other pocket.

MACK. *(Taking it.)* Bit careless with my money, son. You want to watch that if you're working for me.

LARRY. Sorry.

(MACK flicks through the notes.)

MACK. Well, that seems to wrap everything up nicely. Good week's work - wouldn't you say, Dozer?

(Everyone hangs on DOZER'S words.)

DOZER. Yes, boss.

(Relief all round.)

MACK. Right. Dozer and me will leave you now, and take this little lot somewhere safe. I'll be back to pick you up this evening, Mandy love.

MANDY. Yes, Mack.

MACK. Dress up nice. We're going to give Harry the Hammer and his missus a night to remember.

MANDY. Yes, Mack.

MACK. *(As he passes TERRY.)* What are we going to do, son?

TERRY. You're going to.... I haven't the faintest idea.

MACK. Good boy - you're learning. *(To LARRY.)* Might see you later. We'll probably drop in at Luigi's for dinner before going on.

LARRY. (Weakly) Lovely.

(MACK goes to the door, followed by DOZER with the brief case. Turns in the doorway.)

MACK. Tell you what, Tania. You and your talkative boy-friend can join us for the evening. Mandy's got lots of dosh to spend. We'll make it a real party.

(They go. The apartment door closes. TANIA collapses weakly onto the sofa.)

TANIA. I don't believe this! We might as well have a suicide pact.

MANDY. What am I going to do? I've got about four pound fifty on me.

TERRY. You could take Big Mack for a Big Mac.

(Laughs at his own joke until he finds himself nose to nose with MANDY.)

MANDY. Find it funny, do you, Terry? Find it an amusing situation? Well I hope you're laughing when you try to explain to Big Mack that you aren't Tania's boy-friend at all; that Larry *is* Tania's boy-friend; that Larry doesn't work at Luigi's; that you *do* work at Luigi's; that Larry didn't deliver Luigi's money; that you *did* deliver Luigi's money; only you didn't deliver *all* Luigi's money; which is why Larry had to give Big Mack back his own money; which is why I now haven't got any money; because you spent all the bloody money at Big Mack's bloody club!

TERRY. All right, all right. I'll think of something.

TANIA. What, like you did last time? Ask Big Mack if he'll lend you a grand? *(Sits on the sofa.)* I'm sorry you've got into all

this, Larry darling. You're the innocent one here.
    LARRY. *(With a glance at MANDY.)* Er.... Yes.

(TANIA inadvertently finds an end of his tie protruding from under the cushion where MANDY has hidden it, pulls it out and absent-mindedly fiddles with it.)

    TANIA. Looks like it's going to spoil our week-end together.
    LARRY. Don't worry about it.
    TANIA. But I do. I wanted this week-end to be special.
    LARRY. *(Focused nervously on the tie.)* Yes, well....
    TANIA. I mean really special - know what I mean?
    TERRY. (With feeling.) *Yeh!*
    TANIA. Who asked you?
    TERRY. Sorry, I....

(TANIA sees what she has in her hand.)

    TANIA. Here - where did this....?
    MANDY. *(Trying to take it.)* Oh, that must be Gerry's - I'll....
    TANIA. No, it isn't. *(To LARRY.)* This is yours!
    LARRY. No, no, not mine....
    TANIA. Yes it is. I gave it to you on our second date - for your birthday.
    LARRY. It can't be the same.....
    TANIA. I spent half an hour choosing it. I'd know that tie anywhere!
    MANDY. Oh god!
    TANIA. How did that get there?
    LARRY. It, er.... I, er....
    TANIA. *(Replacing the tie and getting to her feet.)* Hold on - the penny's beginning to drop....

MANDY. Oh hell!

TANIA. *(To MANDY.)* You had a new man here....

MANDY. He's gone.

TANIA. Who didn't want to come out of the bathroom....

MANDY. He was caught short.

TANIA. Larry turns up early....

LARRY. Only an hour or two.

TANIA. With the money Terry had given to you....

TERRY. I knew it wouldn't work.

TANIA. But not the tie I gave to him....

TERRY. I said it was daft.

MANDY. Belt up, you!

(TERRY belts up.)

TANIA. Say it's not what I think it is, Mandy.

MANDY. I didn't know who he was, Tania, honest.

TANIA. What d'you mean, didn't know?

MANDY. I didn't know he was yours, I promise. I'd never have got off with him if I'd known.

TANIA. *(Glaring at LARRY.)* He knew!

LARRY. I'm sorry, Tania. I didn't mean it to happen. I like you, I really do.

TANIA. Bloody funny way of showing it!

LARRY. I just fell head over heels for Mandy. It was different. She was....

TANIA. An easy lay.

MANDY. *(Indignant)* I was not!

TANIA. Didn't take long though, did it? Whereas I made you wait for it.

LARRY. It wasn't the waiting.

TANIA. What was it then?

LARRY. It was just.... Chemistry.

TERRY. I don't mind waiting.

TANIA. Do you want a punch in the face?

TERRY. Sorry.

MANDY. I'm so sorry, Tania - really. If I'd known I'd never have talked to him.

TANIA. *(To LARRY.)* You must have had your sights on her right from the start!

LARRY. I just saw her on stage, and I thought....

TANIA. She had better legs than me.

LARRY. No, no - definitely not.

TERRY. Definitely not.

(She raises her fist. He picks up a cushion to defend himself.)

LARRY. Like I said, it was just chemistry. I can't explain it. I didn't want to hurt you.

TANIA. Oh well - there goes another one. I've just got to face it - I scare men off.

TERRY. *(Muttering)* You scare the hell out of me.

TANIA. *(Turning on him and taking him by the ear.)* You haven't seen anything yet, chum!

TERRY. Ow! All right, all right - I'll keep quiet!

TANIA. *(To LARRY.)* Well, I hope you realise what you've got yourself into. Not only are you impersonating one of Big Mack's gang; not only will Big Mack think you've diddled him out of a thousand quid; now you've pinched Big Mack's girl! He's going to have the Bulldozer tear you limb from limb!

LARRY. I know. Oh god!

TANIA. *(To MANDY.)* You started all this, Mandy. How the

hell are you going to get us out of it?
    MANDY. I dunno. Oh, Larry I wish you'd told me who you
were.
    LARRY. I'm sorry. If I'd known it was going to lead to this....
    MANDY. Perhaps if I can get hold of some money for tonight,
we could still get away with it.
    TANIA. Don't be daft.
    MANDY. Why not?
    TANIA. For one thing I'd have to spend the evening pretend-
ing this prat is the love of my life! *(Indicates TERRY.)*
    TERRY. *(Glum)* Well my mother quite likes me.
    TANIA. For another Mack wants us all to have dinner at
Luigi's. How are you going to explain it to Terry's boss?
    TERRY. I could spend a long time in the gents.
    TANIA. For another, Terry owes a grand to Harry the
Hammer, who's going to be with us. How are you going to explain
it to him?
    TERRY. I could grow a moustache.
    TANIA. Are you always such a plonker?
    TERRY. Yeh.
    TANIA. Well keep it to yourself.
    MANDY. Oh god, this is a nightmare!
    TANIA. So is this really a big thing between you two?

(LARRY and MANDY look at each other.)

    BOTH. Yes.
    TANIA. *(Mournful)* Just what I was longing for.
    TERRY. I could put a big thing between us.
    TANIA. *(Raising her eyes to heaven.)* I don't believe this
character.

TERRY. Sorry. I can't help it.

TANIA. *(To MANDY.)* So why don't you both run off together?

MANDY. Big Mack would follow us to the South Pole.

TANIA. All right, I've a better idea.

MANDY. What?

TANIA. The problem is we can't pay for this night out that Mack wants, yes?

MANDY. So?

TANIA. When he arrives, surprise him with a dinner party here instead.

MANDY. Here?

TANIA. Say you wanted to make it a nice intimate celebration for Harry and his wife. Lay on a real spread. That way you don't have to spend his money, and you don't have to visit Luigi's.

MANDY. I've no money for a spread.

TANIA. Order it in.

MANDY. Where from?

TANIA. Um.... Luigi's?

MANDY. Are you crazy??

TANIA. Luigi knows you. Phone him up and put it on Big Mack's account.

MANDY. He never pays it anyway.

TANIA. There you are then.

TERRY. That's good.

LARRY. Yes, that is quite good.

MANDY. It's insane!

TERRY. It's bloody good grub.

MANDY. This is getting worse and worse! If we stay in, then he's going to want the money back he's given me for going out.

TANIA. Say you're keeping it somewhere safe for next time.

TERRY. Hold on. Harry the Hammer will still want his money

back.

LARRY. *(Confused)* What money?

TERRY. The money I borrowed in the first place.

TANIA. That's your problem, chum. If you hadn't done that we wouldn't be in this mess.

TERRY. Don't rub it in.

TANIA. Does Harry know you now work at Luigi's?

TERRY. No.

TANIA. So that's all right. And Mack doesn't like talking business on social occasions, so Harry the Hammer probably won't make a big thing of the money. You'll just have to talk him into waiting a bit longer.

TERRY. Like a couple of years?

MANDY. I suppose it might work.

TANIA. It will if you use your charms on Big Mack.

LARRY. Great. What do I do meanwhile? Sit and twiddle my thumbs elsewhere?

TANIA. Count yourself lucky you've still got thumbs to twiddle, lover boy!

MANDY. Hang on - Mack thinks he's Luigi's boy.

TANIA. So?

MANDY. He could collect the dinner.

LARRY. What?

TERRY. That's my job.

MANDY. Well you won't be there to do it, will you?

LARRY. But Luigi knows him.

MANDY. I'll just tell Luigi I'm sending someone to collect it.

LARRY. Terrific. So I'm a waiter now.

TANIA. We'll give you a good tip.

TERRY. And I've lost my job.

MANDY. Pray that's not all you lose. Right, we'll have to give it a try. This could be our last day on earth, people. Better make the most of it.

LARRY. *(Looking at her.)* Good idea.

MANDY. What? *(Realises his intentions.)* Oh.

TANIA. What? *(Also realises.)* Oh.

TERRY. What? *(Doesn't realise.)* What?

TANIA. Never mind. It's time we left.

TERRY. Why...? *(She just looks.)* Oh, right.

TANIA. *(To MANDY.)* Lucky sod. *(To LARRY.)* Sunday in bed - that's what I was hoping for.

LARRY. *(Remorseful)* Sorry, Tania.

TERRY. You could still have it.

TANIA. *(Shoving him to the door.)* Not a chance!

TERRY. Just offering.

TANIA. I'd rather have Dozer wash my back. Get out of here!

TERRY. You're just playing hard to get. I can tell. *(She smacks him round the head.)* Ow!

TANIA. *(To the others as she goes.)* Why do I always get the wallies? Enjoy yourselves.

(Goes. The door closes. They look at each other.)

MANDY. You realise this could be the last time, Larry.

(He picks her up and carries her to the bed.)

LARRY. They always said the world might end with a big bang.

(Throws her onto the bed, and starts taking off his trousers.)

CURTAIN

ACT II

(Early evening. The light is fading. As at the beginning of Act One, two forms can be detected under the bed clothes on the bed. One stirs, moans, sits up. It is MANDY, looking thoroughly ravaged. She comes to her senses, looks at the time, is galvanised into action.)

MANDY. Oh, God! Oh my God!

(She shakes the form beside her. LARRY'S head appears.)

LARRY. What? Wossup?

MANDY. Larry, it's ten to seven!

LARRY. What's for breakfast?

MANDY. It's evening! We've done it again!

LARRY. Done what?

MANDY. For Christ's sake - we fell asleep! Big Mack 'll be here any moment!

LARRY. *(Wide awake.)* Oh bloody hell!

MANDY. Quick! You must get out of here!

LARRY. *(Pulling on his shorts under the covers.)* What time's he due?

51

MANDY. Now! Oh, Larry, how could we do it again?

LARRY. Because we did it again and again and again. I was nackered.

(Kisses her affectionately.)

MANDY. Well you're not doing it again! Get dressed! *(He jumps out of bed.)* Throw me my robe.

(He picks up the same gaudy bath-robe.)

LARRY. Good grief!

(Throws it to her, and hops around putting on his clothes. The door bell rings.)

MANDY. Oh God, it's them! Quick - in the bathroom!

LARRY. I'm getting so tired of that bloody bathroom.

(He dashes to the bathroom with his clothes. She flings in after him various items he has missed, and closes the bathroom door. Another ring on the door bell. She straightens her hair in the mirror, and hurries to the door. TANIA and TERRY stand there.)

TANIA. Hey, girl, aren't you ready yet?

MANDY. Oh, thank God it's you! Quick, come inside!

(They enter.)

TANIA. What's going on?

MANDY. We aren't ready! We overslept.

TANIA. What again?

MANDY. Yeh, you see, we er... we were, er....

TERRY. We know what you were doing.

TANIA. Why were you doing it now for heaven's sake?

MANDY. We weren't - we were asleep.

TANIA. You slept all day?

MANDY. Well we didn't get much sleep last night, you see, and...

TANIA. What is he, a pedigree bull?

MANDY. Oh Tania, help us please. Mack and Harry the Hammer will be here any second!

TANIA. Where's lover boy?

MANDY. Getting dressed in the bathroom.

TANIA. Why have I got a feeling of deja vu? Well you'd better do the same. You look like a Christmas cracker!

MANDY. *(Hurrying to her collect her clothes.)* Where have you two been anyway?

TANIA. The zoo. I thought he might feel at home there.

MANDY. Oh, so you're friends now?

TANIA. No.

TERRY. She tried to push me in the snake pit!

TANIA. To join the rest of his family.

(MANDY grabs a neat little evening frock from a hook on the door.)

MANDY. I'll dress in the kitchen.

TANIA. What do we say if they turn up? You're supposed to have dinner all ready for them.

MANDY. Order it from Luigi's and I'll set the table in there.

TANIA. Good grief - haven't you ordered it yet? *(Goes to the phone.)* Terry, clear this place up, while I call Luigi's.

TERRY. What am I, a chamber maid?

TANIA. You'll be a bloody chamber pot if you don't do as you're told. Shat on from a great height!

TERRY. *(Grumbling)* All right.

(TERRY straightens the bed and clears up, as MANDY hurries to the kitchen with her clothes, and TANIA taps on the phone.)

TANIA. *(To the phone.)* Luigi? Hello, it's Tania here from Big Mack's place. Mandy's asked me to call and order a takeaway from you. Six people - you know what Big Mack likes to eat - some nice wine - to go on Big Mack's account. *(Looking at TERRY.)* What - the new boy hasn't turned up? Well we'll send someone to collect it. *(Puts the phone down.)*

TERRY. I'll get the sack almost before I've started.

TANIA. That's the least of your worries. *(Goes to the bathroom door, and knocks.)* Hey, stud! Get your skates on - you've got to go and collect the dinner.

LARRY. *(Off)* Coming.

(At that moment the apartment door opens and BIG MACK walks in, followed by HARRY the HAMMER and DOZER. The former is an unsavoury looking character of indeterminate age.)

MACK. Hello, Tania girl. Here we are.

TANIA. Hello, Mack.

MACK. Do you know Harry the Hammer? Known to his friends as Whammy the Slammer - ha,ha. Harry, this is Tania, one of my girls.

HARRY. Tasty.

MACK. Hands off, Harry. *(Introducing TERRY.)* This is her boy-friend, Terry the Mouth. Known to his friends as nothing at all because he hasn't got any - ha, ha.

TERRY. *(Feebly)* Ha, ha.

HARRY. I know you, don't I?

TERRY. Er.... well....

HARRY. You owe us money.

TERRY. Er... yes, I er....

MACK. What?

HARRY. Yeh - he borrowed a thousand big ones.

MACK. Don't tell me you've got in debt, Terry?

TERRY. Well....

MACK. That is a very stupid thing to do.

TERRY. Yes....

MACK. Especially at the outrageous rates Harry charges. I know because I set them.

TERRY. They are a bit strong.

MACK. What did you want it for?

TERRY. Well, er....

MACK. Not hoping to get rich by putting it all in one go on the red, I hope.

TERRY. No, no.

MACK. That would be very stupid, wouldn't it?

TERRY. Yeh.

MACK. Tania, I'm even more disappointed in your choice of boy friends. This lad's got a death wish. What's he want to go borrowing money from shysters like Harry the Hammer for?

TANIA. Silly of him, Mack.

MACK. Certainly is. You'd better give it back as quickly as possible, Terry, before Harry owns you body, soul and scrotum.

TERRY. Yeh.

MACK. Which means I own you. Which means Dozer deals with you. And you know which bit he deals with first.

TERRY. Yeh.

MACK. Right. Where's Mandy?

TANIA. Er.... in the kitchen.

MACK. What's she doing in there? She should be tarting herself up ready to go.

TANIA. Oh she's nearly ready, Mack. Er... where's Harry's wife?

HARRY. She's not coming.

TANIA. Why not?

MACK. She's left him.

TANIA. Oh dear.

MACK. Divorce number five is on its way, isn't it Harry?

HARRY. Yeh.

MACK. Tell you the truth, I'm not surprised. He's horrible to live with.

HARRY. *(Nodding)* Yeh.

MACK. Never mind - we'll celebrate his freedom instead. I'll just go and adjust my make-up and then we can all hit the bright lights, eh?

(Moves towards the bathroom.)

TANIA. *(Quickly)* Oh, Mack, er.... Mandy wanted to tell you something.

MACK. Well she can - after I've done my hair.

TANIA. Well it was rather urgent.

MACK. Why, what's happened?

TANIA. Er.... I think there's been a change of plan. *(Calls)* Mandy!

MACK. Change of plan?

TANIA. Yes.

MACK. I'm the only one who changes plans around here.

TANIA. I think she's got a surprise for you. *(Urgently)* Mandy!

MACK. Has she now? Well that's nice. *(To the bathroom again.)* She can tell me about it after I've....

(MANDY comes out of the kitchen, dressed.)

MANDY. Oh, Mack!

MACK. *(Turning back.)* Hello, Mandy girl.

MANDY. You're in good time.

MACK. Aren't I always?

MANDY. Yes. Hello, Harry.

HARRY. Hello, Mandy.

MACK. Harry's wife won't be joining us. Harry and his wife are no longer an item.

MANDY. Oh.

MACK. As far as Harry's wife is concerned Harry's hammer no longer makes an impact.

MANDY. Oh dear. I'm sorry, Harry.

HARRY. *(Eyeing TANIA.)* I'm not.

MACK. Eyes front, Harry. You're on good behaviour tonight.

HARRY. Why?

MACK. You're supposed to be mourning the demise of your marriage, for Christ's sake!

HARRY. Oh, right.

MACK. God there's no stopping him! Now what's this about a surprise, Mandy girl?

MANDY. Oh, well.... yes, Mack, I just thought that for a change we should do something different.

MACK. Different?

MANDY. We're always going out on the town. I thought for a special occasion like this it would be nice to have a quiet, intimate party here instead.

MACK. Not such a special occasion now, is it?

MANDY. Never mind - we can still have dinner here. I've organised it all.

MACK. That's very forward of you, doll.

MANDY. Well, I just wanted a nice quiet evening with you and me and some friends. I've ordered one of Luigi's specials. It's on its way over. *(Beseeching)* Isn't it, Tania?

TANIA. More or less.

MACK. I see. *(Pause)* Well, why not? Make a change, eh Harry?

MANDY. *(Relieved)* That's what I thought.

MACK. We'll have a cosy evening listening to the stimulating repartee of Harry the Hammer and Terry the Mouth.

HARRY. Yeh.

MACK. To say nothing of Dozer. *(DOZER just grins. MACK turns to the bathroom.)* Now I'll just....

MANDY. *(Quickly)* And er... all that money you gave me, Mack.

MACK. *(Turning)* What about it?

MANDY. I've put it somewhere private. For next time. Just thought you'd like to know.

MACK. Right. Good. Well now I'm going somewhere private to....

(Puts his hand on the bathroom door knob.)

MANDY. *(Desperate)* Mack, er....

MACK. Hello. This door's locked.

MANDY. Er... yes.

MACK. Someone's in there.

MANDY. Er... yes.

MACK. Who?

MANDY. Er... a friend of mine.

MACK. A friend?

MANDY. Yes.

MACK. Who?

MANDY. Just... just a friend.... who's visiting.

MACK. Visiting?

MANDY. Yes. Dropped by.

MACK. Dropped by?

MANDY. Yes.

MACK. How interesting. Isn't that interesting, Dozer? Mandy has a friend dropped by.

DOZER. Yes, boss.

MACK. Well, let's meet this friend, Mandy girl. I always like to meet friends of yours - especially if they've dropped by.

MANDY. Oh well.... they're in the bathroom, and....

MACK. Well, let's get them out of the bathroom. I want to meet them. *(Turns and knocks on the door.)* Hey! Friend of Mandy's! Come out - we want to meet you. *(Knocks again.)* D'you hear me? Come out of there.

(There is the sound of a lock turning. MACK steps back. The door opens slowly and LARRY comes out. He is unrecognisable. He wears a woman's dress and high heels, blonde wig, and heavy make-up - the full drag. He is quite a dish.)

LARRY. *(To MACK.)* What's the matter, big boy?

MACK. *(Taken aback.)* Oh - sorry.... I didn't realise.

LARRY. Can't a girl tart herself up without being interrupted?

MACK. I thought you were, er....

LARRY. Yes?

MACK. Somebody else.

LARRY. Sorry to disappoint you.*(Looking round.)*Well, Mandy - you didn't tell me you were having a party.

MANDY. *(Dumb-struck.)* Um....

LARRY. Who are all these lovely people?

MANDY. Um....

HARRY. *(Coming smartly forward.)* I'm Harry. Harry the Hammer they call me.

LARRY. *(Shaking his hand.)* And why would they call you that, Harry?

HARRY. Well, I....

MACK. Because he's a much-used tool, that's why. But he's getting decidedly worn. So back off, Harry. *(HARRY backs off. MACK steps forward and shakes LARRY'S hand.)* I'm Joe MacAllister - otherwise known as Big Mack, because I'm the big man around here.

LARRY. Oh yes, I've heard about you.

MACK. Nothing good, I hope - ha, ha. I'm Mandy's employer. In fact I'm practically everyone's employer.

LARRY. I'm impressed.

MACK. And who are you?

LARRY. They call me Laura.

MACK. Laura.

LARRY. Otherwise known as Big Lorry, because I'm the big girl around here.

MACK. *(Intrigued)* Oh.

HARRY. Well, Big Lorry, you can run over me any time - ha,

ha.

MACK. *(Turning to MANDY.)* And why hasn't Big Laura been introduced to us before, Mandy?

MANDY. *(Still dazed.)* Er.... well, er....

LARRY. Well I'm not actually from round here. I was just in town for a day or two, and I thought I'd drop by and see how my old friend Mandy was getting on. Seems like I picked a good moment.

MACK. Well, yes indeed. In fact it's lucky for us you've come.

LARRY. Really?

MACK. We were all about to have a party. And we're a bit short on numbers, so Laura can join in and make them up - can't she, Mandy?

MANDY. Er....

LARRY. That's very kind of you, Mack, but I'm afraid I've got a prior engagement.

MACK. *(Disappointed)* Oh dear.

LARRY. In fact I'm late as it is - so if you don't mind....

MACK. Oh but I do, Laura, I do. We can't meet one of Mandy's oldest friends like this without getting to know her a bit. *(To the others.)* We'd love to get to know Laura a bit, wouldn't we fellers?

ALL. *(With enthusiasm.)* Yes, boss, definitely, love to, etc.

MACK. Then that's settled. You can put off your engagement for a bit, I'm sure....

LARRY. Oh, well you see, Mack, it's my boy-friend, and he hates to be kept waiting. He's a very masterful sort.

MACK. Is he? Well I'll tell you what - ask him too.

LARRY. Oh, but....

MACK. There'll be lots for everyone, and we'd love to meet

her boy-friend, wouldn't we, fellers?

ALL. *(With less enthusiasm.)* Yes, boss, definitely, love to, etc.

MACK. Perhaps I can give him a job.

LARRY. He's already got a job, and he lives a long way away, actually, so....

MACK. Oh well, too bad. *(Looks at his watch.)* Tell you what, it's very early - he can't be expecting you just yet. Stay and have a drink with us, Laura, and then we'll let you go to your masterful boy friend. How about it?

LARRY. *(Hesitating)* Well, I don't....

MACK. I insist. Give him a call if necessary, and tell him you'll be a little late.

LARRY. I don't think, er....

MACK. Tell you the truth - I'd love to find out more about Mandy's private life and her friends and all that. I'm very fond of Mandy, you see, but she's quite a secretive girl.

LARRY. Is she?

MACK. *(Leading LARRY to the sofa.)* So, Laura, sit down and let's find something to drink. Have we still got some champagne in the fridge, Mandy?

MANDY. Yes, Mack.

MACK. Good. Pull it out and let's get this party rolling!

MANDY. Er.... right.

(MANDY goes towards the kitchen.)

TANIA. Oh, Mandy - didn't Luigi say he wanted us to collect the dinner?

MANDY. *(Stopping)* Did he?

TANIA. *(Pointedly indicating TERRY.)* I thought he said he was a bit short-staffed.

MANDY. *(Understanding)* Oh, yes.

MACK. Why - what's happened to the new boy?

MANDY. Er.... he hasn't turned up.

MACK. Gawd - staff! You can't trust anyone these days, Laura.

LARRY. It must be a terrible problem, with all your responsibilities.

MACK. Yes, they all think they can take you for a ride. Well he won't do it again. I'll have Dozer teach him a lesson.

(Both TERRY and LARRY react uneasily.)

LARRY. Nothing too drastic, I hope, Mack. The poor boy may have had an accident or something.

MACK. Well if he hasn't he's about to. I've met the poor boy and he's a dick-head.

LARRY. Oh dear.

MACK. Meanwhile, Dozer, take the car round to Luigi's and pick up dinner for us all.

DOZER. Yes, boss.

MACK. And while you're there, ask Luigi what the new boy's full name is and where he lives.

TERRY. *(Muttering)* Oh shit!

MACK. What, Terry?

TERRY. Er... he's in the shit.

MACK. He certainly is. Though it's none of your business. You're in enough of your own.

TERRY. Yes.

(DOZER goes.)

MANDY. I'll get the champagne.

(MANDY goes into the kitchen.)

MACK. *(Indicating TANIA and TERRY.)* Have you met these two, Laura?

LARRY. Yes, I have.

MACK. Tania here's another of my show-girls. All chosen specially for their intellectual accomplishments.

LARRY. I can see that.

MACK. And Terry is her boy-friend. Chosen for I'm not sure what accomplishments, but I don't think they're intellectual.

TERRY. Now look....

MACK. *(Mildly)* Yes, Terry, did you wish to speak?

TERRY. No.

MACK. So, Laura, tell us....

(Tails off as he notices LARRY adjusting his bra, which has slipped somewhat. LARRY smiles feebly.)

LARRY. *(Apologetic)* It's a new bra - I haven't quite got the hang of it yet.

MACK. Tell us, what are your accomplishments? Apart from the obvious ones.

LARRY. Well, Mack.... I'm a professional girl.

MACK. I hope you don't mean that the way I'd mean it, Laura.

LARRY. *(Laughing a girlish laugh.)* Oh no, no. I work in the City.

MACK. Do you now? Not just a pretty face, eh. How very interesting.

LARRY. Oh, it is.

MACK. What particular field in the City - if that's not a contradiction in terms - ha,ha?

LARRY. Ah, you're a wit, Mack. Well, I handle portfolios for a number of clients.

HARRY. You can handle my portfolio any time.

MACK. Shut up, Harry. *(To LARRY.)* So how did someone in your line of business come to make friends with someone in Mandy's line?

LARRY. Oh well, Mack, er.... we go back a long time.

MACK. Really?

LARRY. *(Nodding)* We were at school together.

MACK. Funny - I never thought of Mandy as going to school.

LARRY. Oh Mack, she's a very bright girl.

MACK. I'm not denying that.

LARRY. She'd have to be to hook a man like you.

MACK. Keep talking, Laura - flattery will get you a long way with me. As a matter of fact you could get a long way with me anyway.

LARRY. I could?

MACK. You could be just the sort of girl I'm looking for.

LARRY. Now, Mack....

MACK. Oh, nothing improper, Laura. It's just that I've been thinking for a while that I ought to take some professional advice on my investments. In my business, you see, you generate a lot of, um.... cash.

LARRY. Ah.

MACK. And it's not really sensible to have cash sitting around doing nothing, is it? It should be working for one in legitimate ways.

LARRY. You mean put through the laundry?

MACK. That's one way to describe it. Now if a bright girl like you was able to advise me on such matters then it could turn out to be a very mutually beneficial arrangement, couldn't it?

LARRY. I'm afraid I already have rather more clients than I can handle, Mack.

HARRY. That's all right - we can get rid of some of them for you.

MACK. Shut up, Harry.

LARRY. But I could certainly pass you on to one of my colleagues.

MACK. Ah, not sure about that, Laura. They probably wouldn't be as pretty as you - and you can never have enough pretty girls around, can you?

LARRY. Flattery will get you nowhere with me, Mack.

(MANDY appears in the kitchen doorway with a champagne bottle.)

MANDY. Oh, Mack....

LARRY. Especially when you've got Mandy.

MACK. Of course.

MANDY. Can you give me a hand with this cork.

MACK. *(Scarcely listening.)* Bring it here, love.

MANDY. Oh, well I need you to see if I've got the right bottle and glasses and everything.

MACK. *(Sighing)* There, you see, Laura. You just can't rely on people to do things for you.

(Rises and goes to the kitchen. MANDY frantically gestures behind his back for LARRY to get out.)

MANDY. Sorry, Mack.

(They go off. HARRY promptly takes MACK'S place on the sofa next to LARRY, who is again readjusting his bra.)

HARRY. D'you need a hand with that?

LARRY. No thank you.

HARRY. So, Laura, tell us more about your business. I'm quite involved in that line myself.

LARRY. Investing people's money, Harry?

HARRY. Well, let's say investing money in people. Aren't I, Terry? *(To LARRY.)* Terry here, for instance, owes me eleven hundred quid.

TERRY. A thousand!

HARRY. Oh, I'm sure it's gone up to eleven hundred since we last spoke, Terry. That's what I mean, Laura - getting real returns on your investments.

LARRY. You're evidently a shrewd businessman, Harry.

HARRY. *(Putting a hand on LARRY'S knee.)* And, like Mack, I believe in a hands-on approach to things.

LARRY. *(Putting his hand back.)* That's good, Harry, as long as you keep your hands clean.

HARRY. Oh naturally. *(Replacing his hand.)* My hands are always clean.

LARRY. *(Putting it back.)* You should keep them like that - especially just before dinner.

TANIA. Er.... don't you think you should be moving on, Laura. You're going to be late.

(Waves towards the door.)

LARRY. Oh, I can stay a little longer. It's such good company here - I'm quite enjoying myself.

HARRY. That's nice!

TERRY. *(Muttering)* God almighty!

TANIA. *(Urgent)* But what about your boy-friend, Big Lorry?

LARRY. He can wait a bit. It never does to let men think they own you, Harry.

HARRY. Well no woman's ever let me own them. Five marriages and five divorces so far - ha, ha.

LARRY. What do you do to them?

HARRY. My trouble, Laura, is the grass is always greener. A bit like bank notes. *(Putting his hand back.)* But then I'm always hoping the woman will one day come along who can keep my patch evergreen.

LARRY. *(Replacing his hand.)* Quite a poet. Who would have guessed it?

TERRY. Yugh!

HARRY. Did you say something, my friend?

TERRY. No, Harry - just feeling a bit sick.

HARRY. Well the cure for that is to concentrate your mind on other things. Like the twelve hundred pounds you owe me.

(TERRY raises his eyes to the ceiling.)

TANIA. *(Pointedly)* Well I think that Laura shouldn't be keeping her boy-friend waiting any longer.

HARRY. What's the matter, Tania? Getting jealous of the opposition?

TANIA. I'm getting worried the opposition's going to bite off more than it can chew.

HARRY. Well now, Laura, there's a challenge! *(Putting his arm round LARRY'S shoulders.)* But then you look to me to be a girl who can chew quite a lot.

(LARRY pokes a sharp finger into HARRY'S arm-pit.)

HARRY. *(Withdrawing his arm smartly.)* Ow!

LARRY. *(Acid)* I do have sharp teeth, if that's what you mean, Harry.

HARRY. *(Backing off.)* Nuff said, nuff said.

(MACK and MANDY enter, the latter carrying a tray of half-filled glasses, and the former an open bottle of champagne.)

MACK. Here we are! Lovely bubbly. Harry, I've told you - leave that nice girl alone. Or do you want me to bend your hammer? *(HARRY smartly leaves the sofa. MANDY puts the tray on a side table, and hands round the glasses as MACK pours more champagne.)* Right now everyone, I want you all to have a glass in your hands - because I've got an announcement to make.

MANDY. What, Mack?

HARRY. Sounds exciting.

MACK. This was going to be Harry's anniversary celebration, but in any case I'd planned to make it another kind of celebration too. I have been feeling for a big while now that it's about time Big Mack gave up the big time and the big bachelor life and took the big step to being a responsible citizen and family man.

HARRY. You don't mean you're going legit, Mack?

MACK. No, nothing as drastic as that - ha, ha. But I've had a good run for my money, and I feel it's time I settled down and made a proper home like other people do. So to that end I've decided to ask Mandy to become my wife.

(Stunned pause. Various intakes of breath all round.)

MANDY. Oh, Mack.....

MACK. Well don't look so astonished everyone. Mandy and I

have known each for quite a time now, she's a great bit of totty, and we get on really well together, don't we, girl?

MANDY. Well, yes, but....

MACK. So I'd really like to make you an offer you can't refuse - ha, ha - and ask you to share my life with me.

HARRY. Well isn't that nice.

TERRY. Very touching.

MACK. What do you say?

MANDY. *(Stunned)* Oh Mack, I don't know - I....

MACK. You know I'll keep you in the manner to which you've become accustomed. You'll be a lady of leisure and pleasure - you won't even have to count the envelopes on a Sunday morning any more - ha, ha.

MANDY. *(Looking desperately at LARRY.)* Well, I.... I....

MACK. I can see I've taken you somewhat by surprise, eh?

MANDY. Yes, Mack, you have. I don't know what to say....

MACK. It's no use looking at Laura. She can't answer for you.

MANDY. *(Bemused)* Um....

LARRY. Perhaps I may offer a little word of advice though, Mack.

MACK. Well now, Laura, I don't see what business it is of yours, but....

LARRY. Of course it isn't, but as one of Mandy's oldest friends I know how overwhelmed she must feel. I'm sure she never in her wildest dreams imagined receiving such a proposition from a man such as you.

MACK. Oh.

LARRY. And I'm sure Tania will agree with me when I say that a girl needs a bit of time to digest an amazing proposal like that.

TANIA. *(Dazed)* Um....

LARRY. After all, Mandy has to be sure she's up to the challenge of partnering a man of your achievements and ambitions.

MACK. Course she's up to it! Aren't you, Mandy girl?

MANDY. I - I....

LARRY. You and I know she is, Mack, but perhaps she needs a little time to convince herself. Isn't that so, Mandy?

MANDY. Well, yes, I.... you did rather take me by surprise, Mack.

MACK. Oh, well yes of course. I don't want to rush you, love. Of course, you take your time, and say yes whenever you feel ready.

HARRY. And if you want any advice about getting married, just ask me. I've had lots of practice.

MANDY. It's very.... it's very kind of you, Mack....

MACK. It's not kind - it's what I want. And I always get what I want.

MANDY. Well, yes, I know you do....

MACK. It's what we both want - isn't it?

MANDY. Well, as Larry.... er, as Laura says, Mack, I do need a bit of time to digest it. It's come as such a shock, and....

MACK. There isn't anyone else, is there?

MANDY. *(Quickly)* No, no - nothing like that!

MACK. I'd hate to feel I had any competition.

HARRY. The competition would hate to feel it too.

(TANIA glares at LARRY, who shifts uneasily.)

MANDY. I just need a bit of time.

MACK. You take all the time you need, girl. Just make up your mind before we get to bed tonight - ha, ha. *(MANDY sits in a daze.)* Well now - has that stirred the nuptial feelings anywhere else? Who else wants to get married? Not you, Harry. How about you, Tania, and Terry here?

TERRY. What a good idea, I'll....

TANIA. Definitely not, Mack.

MACK. Oh dear - looks as if you've got to work a bit harder to win her round, Terry. Can't say I blame her though. You're rather too much of a prat for a girl like Tania, wouldn't you say?

TERRY. Why is it everyone sees me like that?

MACK. Right - well, notwithstanding that we haven't exactly set the date yet, I'd like to drink a toast anyway. *(Raises his glass.)* Here's to little Mandy and Big Mack. Long may they be together.

ALL. *(Raising their glasses.)* Mandy and Mack!

(MANDY smiles feebly. LARRY hasn't moved.)

MACK. *(Noticing)* Aren't you going to toast your oldest friend's engagement, Laura?

LARRY. I'm a bit superstitious, Mack. It might be bad luck to do it before Mandy has formally accepted.

MACK. Fair enough.

LARRY. But I'll certainly drink to her. *(Raises his glass.)* Here's wishing you every happiness, Mandy, whatever choice you make. And I think that any man, whoever he may be, would be very happy to have you.

MANDY. Thank you.

TERRY. Even if he's a woman. *(TANIA kicks him.)* Ow!

MACK. *(Frowning)* What did you say?

TERRY. Er.... what I meant was, any woman... whoever they may be, would say that any man... whoever he is, would be happy to have Mandy.... whoever she choses....

(Tails off. Pause.)

MACK. Prat.

MANDY. *(Somewhat shaken.)* Well, if you'll excuse me, I need to.... after all that I.... need some air.....

(Goes off onto the balcony.)

HARRY. *(Calling after her.)* Don't jump off - ha, ha!

MACK. You're asking to be thrown off.

HARRY. Sorry, Mack.

MACK. I'll fetch another bottle of this stuff. I think we're going to need it.

(Goes into the kitchen.)

TANIA. *(Muttering to LARRY.)* Get out of here!

LARRY. Yes. *(Gets up.)* Well, it's been a lovely evening. But I really think it's time I left now.

HARRY. Oh you can't go now, lovely Laura. Things are just warming up.

LARRY. I know, Harry. That's why I should leave now, before they get any hotter.

(Heads for the door, hitching up his bra as he goes.)

HARRY. *(Cutting him off.)* Now come on, Big Lorry, you can't just slip out like that, without even saying goodbye to everyone. Besides I was really looking forward to getting to know you better. You're my kind of girl.

LARRY. If you knew me better, Harry, you wouldn't think I

was your kind of girl.

(TERRY splutters.)

HARRY. *(Advancing)* Oh, but you are. I've had much experience of women, Laura, and I always look for what's beneath the facade.

LARRY. *(Retreating round the sofa.)* I wouldn't want you looking too deep under my facade, Harry.

HARRY. Why? Find a few surprises, would I?

LARRY. You could say that.

TERRY. One or two.

HARRY. Who asked you?

TERRY. Sorry. None of my business.

HARRY. *(Advancing again.)* So - a woman of mystery are you, Laura? That's a challenge.

LARRY. *(Retreating)* Harry....

HARRY. Why don't you sit down with me, and let's see if the Hammer can't unlock some of your nuts and bolts, eh?

LARRY. My nuts and bolts are my own business. *(To TANIA.)* Help me, Tania!

TANIA. You wanted to join in the party - you're on your own now.

LARRY. *(Getting desperate.)* Terry!

TERRY. *(Raising his glass.)* May the best man win.

HARRY. Come on, Laura - give me a chance. You'll find I'm a good man underneath.

LARRY. That's what worries me, Harry - you might find the same about me.

(Just as HARRY appears about to have LARRY pinned down on the sofa, MACK enters with another bottle of champagne.)

MACK. What the bloody hell....! Harry, what's the matter with you? Can't you keep your flaming tool-box closed for two minutes?

HARRY. *(Standing back.)* I was just trying to get to know Laura better.

MACK. Getting to know someone better doesn't mean diving into their Marks and Spencers the moment you've shaken hands!

HARRY. No, well - sorry....

(MANDY comes in from the terrace.)

MANDY. What's going on?

MACK. Harry here's been practising his engineering skills again. You and I can't leave the room for a second, doll, without him losing his thread.

MANDY. Harry, what's the matter with you?

HARRY. Too many Viagra sandwiches.

LARRY. *(Recovering his composure.)* Well it's been a fascinating evening everyone. A thrilling experience, but I really think it's time I was going.

(Heads for the door.)

MACK. *(To HARRY.)* Now see what you've done! You've scared the poor girl away!

HARRY. *(Barring LARRY'S way.)* Please, Laura, I'm very sorry. Don't go. I didn't mean....*(Stops as he notices that as a result of all the activity LARRY'S chest has slipped down around his waist.)* Here - what's happened to your bust?

LARRY. *(Trying to rescue it.)* Oh dear, I....

HARRY. *(Suspicious)* Hang on a minute! *(Grabs at LARRY'S*

wig. It comes off in his hands. LARRY stands exposed. Stunned pause.) Gawd almighty!

TERRY. Oops!

TANIA. Here we go.

LARRY. *(In his own voice, abashed.)* Evening all.

MACK. What the flaming....? Wait a minute - I know who you are! You're Luigi's new boy!

LARRY. No. Er.... yes.

MACK. Make up your mind.

LARRY. Yes. I hadn't thought back that far.

MACK. What the hell are you doing in drag?

LARRY. *(Feebly)* Just though it might liven up the party.

HARRY. Gawd! To think I was trying to pull him!

MACK. You always did have a strange taste in women, Harry. *(To LARRY, menacing.)* What's this all about? Have you been sent to spy on me?

LARRY. No, no....

MACK. Then what are you up to?

LARRY. I.... I....

MACK. *(Advancing)* Yes?

LARRY. The truth is....

MACK. Well?

LARRY. I wanted to impress you.

MACK. *(Stopping)* What?

LARRY. I want to get into show business, you see, and I do this drag act, and I thought - well, if I can show Big Mack what I can do maybe he'll put me in his night club show.

TERRY. *(Muttering)* Nice one.

MACK. *(Suspicious)* Is this on the level?

LARRY. *(Laughing feebly.)* Yes, really. I thought, if I can fool you and your friends, I can fool anybody.

MACK. You said you were a friend of Mandy's.

LARRY. Ah....

MACK. *(To MANDY.)* Were you in on this?

MANDY. I, er.....

LARRY. Yes.... you see, I er.... I confided in Mandy first of all, thinking she could tell me the best way to get to you.

MACK. That true, Mandy?

MANDY. Yes, yes, Mack. I.... I told him you were going to be here tonight, and I thought it might be a good chance to surprise you.... and liven up the party at the same time.

HARRY. He certainly did that.

MACK. Bloody funny way to liven up a party.

MANDY. I just thought it would be a bit of fun. I said he could use my wig and my clothes and stuff.

MACK. *(Staring at LARRY'S dress.)* Gawd yes! I gave you that dress for your birthday!

MANDY. I thought it looked rather good on him.

MACK. *(To TANIA.)* You know about this, Tania?

TANIA. Er.... yes, Mack. I thought you'd quite appreciate the joke.

MACK. *(Indicating TERRY.)* And did laughing boy know?

TERRY. *(Shaking his head.)* No, er.... *(Sees MANDY nodding. Turns the shake into a nod.)* Yes.

MACK. Yes or no, which is it?

TERRY. I wasn't sure if I was meant to or not, but I did, yes. Good laugh, I thought.

MANDY. You must admit, Mack - he did have you fooled.

TANIA. *(Dry)* He certainly had Harry fooled.

MACK. *(Softening)* Yeh, well.... *(Looks at HARRY.)* He had you on heat, Harry, that's for sure! Heh, heh. He had your hammer waving all right - ha, ha. *(General relaxing all round, except for HARRY.)* My God, I'd love to have seen your reaction when you started groping his fundamentals! Ha, ha. Thought marriage number six was on the horizon, didn't you, Harry? Well that would have been a short engagement, that's for sure!

(He is now roaring with laughter. Everyone except HARRY joins in.)

HARRY. All right, all right. It's not that funny.

MACK. Oh yes it is, Harry! You pride yourself on your knowledge of women. Well I've never seen you get such hot trousers in such a short space of time - and all over a lad who's probably got a hammer that makes yours look like a toothpick! Ha, ha! *(General hilarity all round.)* Harry the Hammer chasing a toyboy round the sofa! Oh you'll never live this one down, Harry. The whole of London will be in hysterics when it gets around!

HARRY. *(Losing his cool.)* All right, all right! I wasn't the only one. He had you fooled just as much as me!

MACK. Ah, but we just talked stocks and banking, Harry, not chicks and bonking.

(More hilarity.)

HARRY. *(Furious)* Well how was I to know? He's just like a bloody girl - look at him. He's probably a poofter anyway!

MACK. *(Sobering)* That's a point. Are you a poofter, son?

LARRY. *(Glancing at MANDY.)* Er.... yes. I'm gay, yes - definitely.

(TERRY splutters.)

HARRY. There you are! See, anyone could have been had.

MACK. Oh, I see. Because he's gay means it was all right to go after his knickers? Well, that says even more about you, my son. Harry the Hammer's given up on marriage - now he's trying his hand at the gay scene! That's going to have everyone in total stitches, that is!

(Hysteria all round. HARRY gets even more furious.)

HARRY. Shut up, shut up! It's not funny! It's bloody sick, that's what is! Going round posing as a female! Trying to seduce fellers - it's bloody perverted!

MACK. You were the one doing the seducing, it seemed to us, Harry.

HARRY. *(Shouting)* Well how was I to know?! She'd got everything in the right place - until it slipped! It wasn't my fault!

(There is a knock on the door. Everyone freezes. Another knock.)

DOZER. *(Off)* Boss - it's me.

MACK. It's Dozer. *(Calls)* Have you got the dinner, Dozer?

DOZER. Yes, boss.

(MANDY goes towards the door.)

MACK. Hold on, Mandy.

MANDY. *(Stopping)* What?

MACK. How about a bit of fun? *(To LARRY.)* You say you want to join our cabaret, eh, son?

LARRY. Er... yes.

MACK. Do you sing in drag, and all that?

LARRY. Oh, yes.

MACK. Well I'll tell you what. You do a proper audition for us. You make up to Dozer, sing us a song and give the Bulldozer a hot flush without him cottoning on, and I'll give you a spot in the show. What d'you say?

LARRY. Ah well, I don't know about that....

MACK. I'll also overlook the little matter of your skiving off work from Luigi's - which I might point out is a capital offence in my outfit.

LARRY. I wouldn't know what to sing.

MACK. You told us you were desperate to get into show-biz. You must know some numbers.

HARRY. Yeh, come on - sing for your supper, Big Lorry.

(LARRY glances at MANDY who surreptitiously urges him on.)

LARRY. *(Reluctant)* Well all right....

MACK. Good. This'll be fun. Get your wig on. *(Calls)* Just coming, Dozer!

(LARRY dresses up again with MANDY and TANIA'S help.)

LARRY. *(Muttering)* I can't do this.

MANDY. *(Ditto)* Yes, you can. Just carry on where you left off.

TANIA. And pray Dozer isn't as randy as Harry the Hammer.

LARRY. *(In despair.)* Oh great!

MACK. *(By the door.)* Right. Everyone ready? I'll do the introductions.

(He opens the door. DOZER enters carrying two large carrier bags.)

DOZER. Dinner, boss.

MACK. Give it to Mandy. (*MANDY takes the bags to the kitchen, and returns immediately.*) We've got a new addition to the party, Dozer. (*Indicating LARRY.*) This is an old friend of Mandy's. She's called Laura.

DOZER. Oh.

LARRY. (*Diffident*) Hi.

MACK. Laura's a cabaret artist. You're just in time to see what she can do, Dozer. She's about to sing a song for us, aren't you, Laura.

LARRY. Yes.

MACK. And there's something else you ought to know about her, Dozer. She likes big men. Don't you, Laura? (*LARRY nods. TERRY splutters. TANIA kicks him.*) The bigger the better. So you're in with a chance here. (*DOZER grins sheepishly.*) Right. Over to you, Laura. Say hello to Dozer.

(*LARRY hesitates. The others start clapping and humming the introduction to 'Hello Dolly'. LARRY slinks around DOZER.*)

LARRY. (*Singing*) Well hello, Dozer....

DOZER. (*Grinning*) Hello, Larry.

(*Collapse of pretence. Astonishment all round. LARRY tears off his wig and flings it down.*)

MACK. How the bloody hell....?

HARRY. He knew! He must have known before!

MACK. Did you know, Dozer?

DOZER. Know what?

MACK. That it was him.

DOZER. No.
MACK. Then how could you tell?
DOZER. I've seen 'Some Like It Hot'.
TANIA. Well done, Dozer - not so stupid, eh?

*(TERRY is in hysterics. BIG MACK becomes aware and turns to
him slowly. TERRY clutches at him, helpless. Then realizes.)*

MACK. You know, I'm becoming very tired of this character.
In fact I'm wondering what on earth a girl like you, Tania, is doing
with such a pillock. Something smells decidedly off round here.
Are you really serious about him?
TANIA. Not really, Mack.
MACK. I'm very pleased to hear it. But I'm puzzled.
TANIA. Why?
MACK. As you know, I like to keep abreast of everything that
goes on in my little empire. Now word has it around the club that
you'd met the love of your life, who's a whizz-kid in the City. So
if that's true, what are you doing with this piece of cold haddock?
TERRY. A lot of people like haddock.
TANIA. The love of my life turned out to be unavailable.
MACK. Why? Who is he?
TANIA. No-one you'd know, Mack.
MACK. I know everyone. Who is he?
TANIA. *(Hesitating)* Well if you really want to know, it's
Larry.
MACK. *(Turning to LARRY.)* Larry!
LARRY. Oh lord!
TANIA. But as you know, he's gay. So he's a lost cause.
MACK. I'm still in the dark, Tania girl.
TANIA. Why?

MACK. Larry's only just started working at Luigi's. So how did you get to know him?

TANIA. Ah. Well....

MACK. Yes?

TANIA. I knew him before.

MACK. Coincidence. Where are you from, Larry?

LARRY. Er.... Hampshire.

MACK. *(Turning to DOZER.)* Did you ask Luigi about the new boy like I told you to, Dozer?

DOZER. Yes, boss.

MACK. And is he Larry from Hampshire?

DOZER. No, boss.

MACK. Then who is he?

DOZER. Terry from Clapham.

MACK. *(Deliberating)* Terry from Clapham.... interesting. *(Turns slowly to TERRY.)* Where are you from, Terry?

TERRY. Er.... Somerset.

MACK. *(Deadpan)* Where are you from, Terry?

TERRY. Er.... near enough.... roundabouts.... not far from.... Clapham.

MACK. Well, well, well - fascinating situation we've got here. Eh, Mandy girl?

MANDY. Yes, Mack.

MACK. We've got an idiot from Clapham who appears to work for Luigi, yet pretends he works in the City, yet for some reason needs to borrow a thousand quid from Harry the Hammer, and who's chasing Tania's knickers. We've got a smoothie from Hampshire, who pretends he works for Luigi, who then pretends he's a girl from your old school who works in the City, who then turns out to be a fairy from Petticoat Lane who'd like to work for me - who's knickers Tania's chasing. And in the middle there's you and me, who aren't pretending to be anyone, and who aren't after anyone else's knickers, I hope, and Harry the Hammer, who doesn't know who the hell he is and who's after everyone's knickers. What do you make of it all?

MANDY. Um....

MACK. Tania, can you throw any light on the situation?

TANIA. Um....

MACK. I think we'd better get to the bottom of all this. I think I need to talk to these two bright sparks separately. Dozer?

DOZER. Yes, boss.

MACK. Take Tony Curtis here to the bathroom, and see he gets out of all that poncy gear - while Terry the Twat and me have a little talk in here.

DOZER. Yes, boss.

MACK. Then they can swap places and we'll see if their stories coincide. *(DOZER and LARRY go off to the bathroom. MACK puts a chair in the centre of the room.)* Harry - sit our friend down there, and get out your carving knife.

HARRY. *(Happily)* Yeh, right.

(Pushes TERRY to the chair, and pulls out a nasty looking folding knife.)

MANDY. Oh, Mack....

MACK. Quiet, Mandy. This is man's business. We'll hear your version later. *(Turns to TERRY.)* Now then, chum. I'm going to ask you a few questions. And every time I hear an answer I don't quite believe, Harry the Hammer is going to cut off a little bit of meat to add to the very nice dinner Luigi's provided for us. Do you understand?

TERRY. I'm a vegetarian actually.

MACK. And every time you make a silly remark that doesn't make me laugh, he'll cut off another bit, all right?

TERRY. Right.

MACK. Right. Now - question number one. Where do you work?

TERRY. Luigi's - if I've still got a job.

MACK. Good. Question number two. *(Indicates TANIA.)* Are you, or have you ever been this girl's boy-friend?

TERRY. Well, I'd like to be...*(HARRY raises his knife.)*...but no.

MACK. Question number three. Did Luigi give you twelve thousand in cash last night to bring to Mandy here?

TERRY. Yes.

MACK. We're doing very well so far, Terry.

TERRY. Good. Can we stop now?

MACK. 'Fraid not. Question number four - why did you want to borrow a thousand quid from Harry?

TERRY. To buy a car.

MACK. Not to gamble at roulette by putting the whole lot on the red?

TERRY. *(Hesitating)* Oh no, no. I wouldn't be that stupid.

MACK. I'll reserve judgement about that. Well now.... final question - and this is the big one, Terry my friend - why, when we arrived here this morning, were you introduced as Tania's feller, and Larry in there as Luigi's boy, and how come he had all Luigi's money?

TERRY. That's three questions.

(HARRY raises the knife.)

TERRY. *(Hurriedly)* All right, all right! I.... er.... I'm not quite sure actually. *(HARRY raises his knife again.)* But I think.... I think you should ask Mandy.

(MACK turns slowly to MANDY.)

    MACK. Mandy?

(Everyone waits agog.)

    MANDY. Ah. Well you see, Mack.... the thing is....that Larry spent the night here with me.
    TERRY. Blimey.

(Pregnant pause.)

    MACK. What?
    MANDY. You see - what happened was this. Larry works in the City, although he'd really like to work in show-business, and Tania met Larry and fell for him, and Larry went out with her for a while because she is in show-business. Then last night Larry came to the club to see Tania, not knowing it was Tania's night off, so Larry went and had a flutter at roulette instead and lost a grand on the red, and then I met him, and Larry told me how upset he was because he didn't know how to tell Tania he was really gay - and Larry had nowhere to go as he'd lost all his money - and so I felt sorry for him, and I said he could sleep here on the sofa. Than Terry brought me the money from Luigi, and Larry and I went to sleep, me in the bed and Larry on the sofa. But in the morning we over-slept, and Tania woke us up, and I was so scared you'd find me with a man in the flat that I told Tania and Larry to pretend that Larry was Terry, who'd turned up late with Luigi's money. But then Terry did turn up late because he'd forgotten to give me the

extra thousand Luigi had given him, and Tania knew Larry was going to come out of the bathroom with Luigi's money, pretending to be Terry, so she introduced Terry as Larry. Then Larry did come out with the money so we introduced Larry as Terry, and Larry gave the money to you. But he couldn't give you all the money because Terry had the rest of it, so then Terry gave the rest of it to Larry too, and Larry gave it to you too, and so there we were.

(Long pause. MACK thinks about it.)

    MACK. Does that make sense, Harry?
    HARRY. *(Also thinking.)* I think so.
    MACK. No loose ends there?
    HARRY. I don't think so.
    MACK. *(To MANDY.)* Larry spent the night here?
    MANDY. Yes.
    MACK. On the sofa?
    MANDY. Yes.
    MACK. All night?
    MANDY. Yes.

(MACK goes to the sofa and picks up LARRY'S tie from where TANIA has left it.)

    MACK. This his tie?
    MANDY. Yes.
    HARRY. It looks like a poofter's tie.
    TANIA. I gave it him for his birthday.
    MACK. Right. *(Calls)* Dozer! Bring our fairy friend back in here. *(DOZER and LARRY enter, the latter changed back into his own clothes.)* Sit him down there. *(LARRY changes places with*

TERRY.) **Right** then, let's have your answers, and anything that doesn't tally, Harry, cut off an appendage.

　　HARRY. Right.

　　MACK. *(Indicating MANDY and TERRY.)* **And** no looking at them - right? *(LARRY nods, unhappily.)* So - you're Larry from Hampshire, yes?

　　LARRY. Yes.

　　MACK. And you work in the City, yes?

　　LARRY. Yes.

　　MACK. So how did you get involved with this bunch of tossers?

(TANIA has positioned herself behind BIG MACK so that neither he nor HARRY sees her. DOZER can, but says nothing during what follows. In fact he quite enjoys it.)

　　LARRY. Er.... *(He sees TANIA in the background pointing at herself.)* I met Tania.

　　MACK. And you started going out with her?

(TANIA nods.)

　　LARRY. Yes.
　　MACK. Are you still going out with her?

(TANIA shakes her head.)

　　LARRY. No.
　　MACK. Why not?

(TANIA makes a camp gesture.)

LARRY. Because I'm gay.
MACK. Where were you yesterday evening?

(TANIA gyrates.)

LARRY. At the club.
MACK. Why? It was Tania's night off.

(TANIA taps her head and shakes it.)

LARRY. I, er.... I didn't know that.
MACK. So what did you do at the club?

(TANIA gambles by dealing cards.)

LARRY. I played cards.
MACK. Cards?

(TANIA frantically indicates a wheel.)

LARRY. And roulette!
MACK. And what happened at roulette?

(TANIA puts thumbs down.)

LARRY. I lost.
MACK. How much?

(TANIA holds up ten fingers.)

LARRY. Ten....*(She frantically points upwards.)*....er, hundred. A thousand.

MACK. How did you lose it?

(TANIA holds up a red finger nail and points to it.)

LARRY. On the red.
MACK. Right. Now the big one, Larry. Where did you sleep last night?
LARRY. Last night?
MACK. That's right.

(TANIA points both fingers at the floor.)

LARRY. Here - on the floor.
MACK. *(Frowning)* Floor?

(She frantically points at the sofa.)

LARRY. Well.... the sofa really - but I ended on the floor - ha, ha.
MACK. Where was Mandy?

(TANIA points at the bed.)

LARRY. In the bed.
MACK. Why would a rich City boy like you want to sleep on Mandy's sofa?

(TANIA indicates empty pockets and sad face.)

LARRY. *(Not understanding.)* I was lonely.... *(She rubs her fingers and thumbs indicating no money.)....* and skint.

MACK. Did you leave anything behind on the sofa?

(TANIA indicates a tie.)

LARRY. My tie.
MACK. *(Producing it.)* Would this be it?
LARRY. That's it!
MACK. Where did you get this tie?

(TANIA points at herself.)

LARRY. Tania gave it to me...*(She nods encouragement and blows out candles.)*...for my birthday.
MACK. So finally, Larry, why, when I and Dozer arrived this morning, did you pass yourself off as Luigi's boy?
LARRY. *(At a loss.)* Ah.... well .....*(TANIA is thinking frantically. HARRY approaches with the knife. TANIA points at him and acts frightened.)*....I was scared...*(She indicates all of them and shakes.)*....we were all scared....*(She points at LARRY and MANDY, and makes lewd copulating gestures.)*... that you'd think Mandy and I had spent the night together....*(She indicates him and TERRY and revolves her fingers.)*....so Terry and I changed places.

(She does thumbs up. Everyone relaxes.)

MACK. Right. Well.... that seems to add up - luckily for you.
HARRY. What a shame.
MACK. But I can't say I'm best pleased.
HARRY. Good. Shall I do him anyway?
MACK. I don't like the idea that everybody has been leading me up the garden path. Especially you, Mandy. Two people who

are getting married ought to be able to trust each other, don't you think?

MANDY. Well, yes, Mack - but you do frighten people.

MACK. I don't frighten you.

MANDY. Yes, you do.

MACK. Do I?

LARRY. Which is why she shouldn't marry you.

MACK. *(Turning with menace.)* What?

LARRY. *(Nervously)* Er... well, its no business of mine....

MACK. No, it's not.

LARRY....but as I'm gay, and a disinterested party as it were - it just seems to me that if there are two people and one wants to marry the other, and the other is so frightened that the other might think there's another, then it's not a very good for either to marry the other.... even if there isn't another....

(Pause)

MACK. Do you follow that, Harry?

LARRY. Harry should know. He's lost five wives.

HARRY. Yeh. I was scared of them all.

MACK. Mandy shouldn't be scared of me. I wouldn't hurt her.

MANDY. Yes, you would, Mack - if you found me with someone else.

MACK. That's different. You wouldn't go with anyone else.

MANDY. You thought I would. You just proved it.

MACK. Ah, well.... Here, are you turning me down?

MANDY. Well I think we ought to wait.

MACK. What for?

MANDY. To make sure I needn't be frightened of you. I think Larry's right.

HARRY. He's buggered you, Mack.

MACK. He what?

HARRY. *(Hastily)* I mean, he's scuppered you. *(Waves the knife.)* Shall I do him?

MANDY. There, you see? The moment anyone says anything you don't like, you have Harry or Dozer do them over!

MACK. *(Reluctantly)* Not really.

MANDY. Yes, you do.

MACK. It's all talk.

MANDY. What?

MACK. Dozer wouldn't hurt a pussy-cat, would you, Dozer?

DOZER. I like cats.

MACK. And Harry faints at the sight of blood.

HARRY. Shhh - don't tell them!

MACK. They just like everyone to think they're tough.

TERRY. *(At HARRY.)* Grrrr!

(HARRY jumps back.)

MANDY. Well they may not be, but you are. And it's not nice living with all these threats around.

MACK. I'll change, Mandy love - I promise.

MANDY. Promises aren't enough.

MACK. We've got champagne and dinner all ready to celebrate.

MANDY. Well we can still have a party. It's up to you to make it a nice one - for everybody.

MACK. *(With bad grace.)* All right.

(MANDY raises her champagne glass.)

MANDY. Good, that's that then. Cheers everyone.

(Relaxation all round. Everyone heads for their glasses.)

MACK. So now you can give me back my thousand.

(Everyone stops.)

MANDY. What?

MACK. The grand I gave you to spend tonight. You won't be wanting it now.

MANDY. *(Hesitating)* Oh. Er....

MACK. You said you'd put it somewhere safe.

MANDY. Yes.... well....

MACK. You haven't lost that, have you?

HARRY. Perhaps she put it on the red - ha, ha.

MACK. Shut up, Harry. *(To MANDY.)* Well?

MANDY. I'd rather hoped you'd forgotten about that.

MACK. I never forget about money. *(Pregnant pause. MANDY is at a loss.)* Put her in the chair, Harry. *(HARRY puts MANDY in the chair. MACK holds out his hand.)* Give me the knife.

HARRY. *(Hesitating)* Oh now, Mack....

MACK. Give me the knife, Harry. *(HARRY hands it over.)* Now then, Mandy. I don't faint at the sight of blood. Where's my thousand?

MANDY. You said you'd never hurt me, Mack.

MACK. That's because I thought you were on my side.

MANDY. I am.

MACK. People who lose my money aren't on my side. Where is it?

(Holds up the knife threateningly.)

TERRY. I'll tell you where it is.

(MACK turns slowly.)

MACK. Well, well - Terry the Mouth has said something interesting at last. Well, Terry?

TERRY. I'll tell you - if you tell me something first.

MACK. What?

TERRY. I'm fascinated, you see, Big Mack. I've always wanted to know how a man like you gets where he is. I mean, I've been trying to do it for years, but I always make a balls-up.

MACK. Yeh, well....

TERRY. How do you get all these smooth businesses and make all this cash?

LARRY. Yes, I'd like to know that too.

MACK. Why?

LARRY. I work my socks off and I do all right, but I'm never in charge of my life. How do you get to run your own empire like you do?

TERRY. Create your own system?

LARRY. Control your own destiny?

MACK. *(Flattered)* You really want to know, lads?

TERRY. Yes.

LARRY. Yes.

MACK. Well I'll tell you. You see, boys, the secret is never answer to anyone. Not your competitors, not your bank manager, not the tax-man....

TERRY. Not the law?

MACK. There are even ways round the law, Terry my friend -

if you're clever enough.... which in your case might be doubtful.

TERRY. How?

MACK. There are a few basic rules - I'll tell you them for free. Rule number one - always think a step ahead of everyone else. If it's the opposition, don't let them do you first; if it's the tax man, don't let him know what you're making; if it's the law, don't let it know what you're doing.

LARRY. That's good.

MACK. Rule number two - don't let anyone know where your money is. If it's on deposit, have it in another name; if it's not legitimate put it through something that is legitimate; and best of all turn it into cash and spend it as fast as you can.

TERRY. That's very good.

MACK. And final rule number three. Don't ever let anyone ever think they can ever get away with ever doing you out of a single penny. So now, Terry, you were about to tell me about my thousand pounds.

TERRY. Yes.

(MACK puts the knife to MANDY'S throat.)

MACK. Go ahead. The future of the evening is in your hands.

TERRY. Well, Mack, the truth is that your thousand pounds has had a very interesting journey.

MACK. Go on.

TERRY. First of all I borrowed it, because I wanted to find out about your loan-shark operations. Then I replaced it out of Luigi's cash because I wanted to find out about your tax evasion operations. Then I gambled it in your club because I wanted to find out about your gaming operations. And finally I borrowed it back from Mandy because I didn't want you to find out about my operations.

MACK. *(Frowning)* What operations?

TERRY. *(Producing an identification.)* Police operations. I'm C.I.D. and you're nicked.

(Pandemonium)

HARRY. Oh my God!

MANDY. Oh, Terry!

TANIA. Wowie - that's good!

MACK. Dozer - get him!

DOZER. *(Hesitating)* Oh no, boss - he looks too tough for me.

MACK. Harry - get him!

HARRY. Sorry, Mack - I'm not tangling with the law!

(MACK puts the knife to MANDY'S throat.)

MACK. I'm warning you! I'll cut her!

(LARRY calmly takes the knife away from behind.)

LARRY. No, you won't.

MACK. *(Whirling)* What?

LARRY. *(Producing an identification.)* I'm a tax inspector, and you're nicked again.

(More exclamations all round.)

MACK. Bloody hell! This is a con job!

TERRY. Too right, Mack. Caught at your own game. *(Pulls aside his jacket to reveal a recording device.)* And we've got all your testimony on tape, so I think that about wraps it up. Dozer and

Harry too. Sorry lads.

    HARRY. Shit!

    DOZER. Oh.

    TERRY. (To LARRY.) Do you want to take them, or shall I?

    LARRY. You take them. I've got some unfinished business here.

    TERRY. Right - downstairs everyone.

    MACK. What makes you think we'll come?

(There is a screech of tyres outside and a blue light flashes on the ceiling.)

    TERRY. Your rule number one, Mack - always think a step ahead of everyone else.

(Waves the three men ahead to the door.)

    HARRY. *(To MACK.)* This is all your fault, Mack.

    MACK. You what? *(Pushes HARRY to the door.)* Don't give me lip, you useless tool!

    DOZER. *(Grabbing MACK by the collar.)* Hey - don't bully Harry! He's a nice man.

    MACK. *(As DOZER marches him to the door.)* Oh God - there's no respect any more. Put me down, Dozer - put me down....!

(The three exit. TERRY turns to TANIA and MANDY.)

    TERRY. Thank you, girls, for a very entertaining day. I haven't had such fun for a long time.

    TANIA. You were very good, Terry - I'd never have guessed.

TERRY. Your trouble is, you play too hard to get, Tania.

TANIA. You should have told me who you were.

TERRY. I'll see you tomorrow and show you all my credentials.

(She smiles. They all leave.)

MANDY. *(Giggling)* You and a copper - that's a funny one!

TANIA. Not as funny as you and a tax inspector.

MANDY. *(To LARRY.)* Yeh - you said you worked in the City dealing with lots of money!

LARRY. I do.

MANDY. Bloody hell - I'll never live it down!

LARRY. What's wrong with being a tax inspector?

MANDY. Not very sexy, is it?

LARRY. *(Advancing)* Ah, you don't know all my investigatory techniques.

MANDY. *(Retreating)* Now, Larry....

LARRY. You haven't seen all my fiscal tools.

MANDY. I thought I had.

LARRY. You haven't had me check all your entries.

MANDY. Oh God, not again, Larry.

TANIA. *(Going to the door.)* You make your entries, I'll make my exit. Just remember to set the alarm this time - Mandy's got a show in twenty four hours.

(She goes.)

MANDY. *(Putting the sofa between her and LARRY.)* Don't you think we should give it a rest, Larry? Let's have a quiet evening.

LARRY. *(Advancing)* We don't have to be noisy about it.

MANDY. *(Retreating)* There's dinner for six in there - it'll go to waste.

LARRY. That's all right - we'll have inter-course intercourse.

MANDY. Larry! You're a sex maniac!

LARRY. I'm a tax inspector. Our motto is 'be upright at all times'.

(Charges at her, and rugby tackles her onto the bed in a flurry of squeals and giggles.)

CURTAIN

PROPERTY LIST

ACT ONE
Day clothes (MANDY & GERRY)
Bright tie (sofa)
Bed linen
Bed cover or duvet
Bath robe (MANDY)
Telephone
Hair brush & cosmetics
Brief case (BIG MACK)
Envelope with bank notes
Mobile phone (LARRY)
Wad of bank notes (BIG MACK)
Sofa cushions
Evening frock (MANDY)

ACT TWO
Slinky female outfit (LARRY)
Wig (LARRY)
Padded bra (LARRY)
2 bottles champagne
Tray with 6 champagne glasses
2 carrier bags (DOZER)
Folding flickknife (HARRY)
2 I.D. cards (TERRY & LARRY)
Miniature recorder (TERRY)

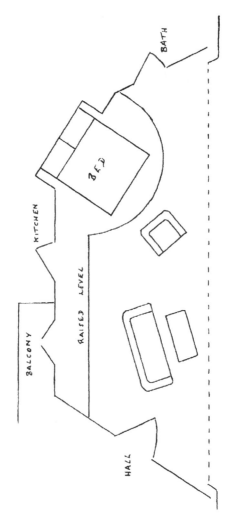

SHADY BUSINESS - Example Ground Plan (Not to scale)

9 780573 622571